HER CYBORG LUMBERJACK

SUSAN HAYES

SUSAN HAYES

Her Cyborg Lumberjack (Book 7 of the Drift: Haven Colony)

First Print: February 2024

Editor: Amanda Brown

Published by: Black Scroll Publications Ltd.

ABOUT THE BOOK

Birds were her only passion... until she met him.

Rin has dedicated her life to the study of birds. When the military uncovers a lost project that results in a new avian species, they hire Rin to investigate what they've created... and how to best use their newest assets.

Rin wants more for her subjects than a life of risk and servitude, but keeping secrets from the military is a dangerous game... especially when playing alone.

This cyborg thought he was better off on his own... then he found her.

Infantry scout. Prisoner. Unwilling test subject. Axe has been many things in his life, but most of it he spent alone.

Freedom hasn't changed that. He protects the colony from a distance, patrolling the wild places others avoid.

He thought he had everything he needed until a chance encounter changes everything. Now he's got a psychic hawk in his head and a bright and cheerful scientist slipping past his walls and into his heart.

She needs his protection. The psy-hawks need his help. And Axe is about to discover that a life of solitude isn't what he wants after all.

PROLOGUE

Beyond the edge of civilized space is a newly colonized planet. It's a haven for the homeless, the hopeful, and those dreaming of freedom.

The beings who live here might be different species from vastly different worlds - but they all have one thing in common. Whoever they are, and wherever they came from, Haven is now their home.

The land is uncharted. The dangers are unknown. It's a world full of possibilities – for those willing to risk everything.

Welcome to Haven Colony.

1

___

Rɪɴ sᴛᴏᴏᴅ by the door inside her habi-pod and waited. When the signal came, she wouldn't have long to make her escape unseen. That knowledge had her nerves on edge and her body keyed up with tension.

A sudden sense of urgency filled her mind, accompanied by a mental projection of the camp. No one was in sight.

"Thanks, Hera," she sent the thought to her companion, and then she was on the move.

She dashed through the door and darted around the corner of her pod without being seen. Once she was out of sight, she resettled her backpack and forced herself to slow down to a brisk walk before emerging into view again. Running would only attract attention, and attention was the last thing she needed. The goal was to get out of camp without being noticed. If Lieutenant Douglas caught her sneaking out against his standing orders...

She didn't dwell on what would happen if the asshole

officer found out what she was up to. Did the military even realize what a jerk they'd put in charge of their precious project?

Don't let him get to you. He's a bully, and bullies aren't worth your time. Her mother had given her that advice long ago when she'd been young and naïve enough to think that dealing with bullies was only something kids had to face.

The camp wasn't large, but for some reason the handful of temporary structures had been placed far apart. The lieutenant said the open areas were part of camp's defenses. She hadn't bothered to point out that they were less than five kilometers away from the colony of Haven. The only thing they'd had to defend themselves from so far was an invasion of rodents the locals called squeakers.

The only reason they were outside the city limits at all was because the Interstellar Armed Forces were afraid their soldiers would fall under the sway of alien pheromones. Rin snorted. Like a female of any species would want to be mated to the males assigned to *this* project.

Not that the aliens got any say about it. The Vardarian mating bond was triggered by chemistry, not choice. You got who you got, and that was the end of it.

She knew the risks when she signed on to this project. If she wound up mated to a pair of Vardarian males, she'd likely lose her job and the lieutenant would step up as project leader. Douglas had already made it clear that the moment he was in charge, he'd terminate the entire experiment and leave. In his opinion this entire mission was a waste of time and resources. At least, that's what he declared once they were safely on their way and out of earshot of anyone who outranked him. *The jerk.*

Rin walked with a steady, purposeful stride toward the building they'd designated as the mews. Inside were five of the six subjects they were here to study. The sixth was perched on the roof of the building, acting as Rin's lookout.

To reach the mews, she had to pass uncomfortably close to the large building the soldiers had claimed as their barracks and mess. She'd timed things so that Douglas and his off-duty men should be having lunch inside. She rarely ate with them, so no one would expect her to show up.

She made it past the open door of the barracks without being seen, but she heard what they were saying. The topic was women. Again.

"I hear the Vardarian females are all randy as hell. It's not *fraxxing* fair that we're not even allowed in the colony." Sutherland had complained about the rules every day since they'd arrived.

"No way I'd hit that. They've got scales! Fucking one of them would be like doing it with a snake," Tao said.

"There are human women in town, too," Sutherland argued. "And bars. And restaurants! Instead we're stuck out here with nothing to do but drill, train, and use the rats for target practice."

Rin had tried to stop that barbaric practice, but Douglas had waved off her concerns and told her the men needed something to do. Plus, the pests were making a mess of the camp, their equipment, and their food supply.

He'd only made two concessions. The first was to ban target practice while the psy-hawks were out of their cages. They were far too valuable to risk injuring. The other was to clear away the dead rats littering the camp. She had no idea where they'd put the bodies, but at least they weren't underfoot anymore.

She made it to the side of the building, but the conversation from inside was still audible thanks to the open vents high on the walls.

"The women in town are all alien-lovers and freaks," Douglas said, his tone venomous. "Why else would they volunteer to come to this planet? No human men are around, just aliens and freakish cyborgs."

"You're forgetting about that kid, Cameron. He's human," Tao said.

Douglas made a derisive noise. "And he's living with two aliens. Like I said, they're all alien-loving freaks."

Rin was tempted to storm inside and give them all a piece of her mind. They were closed-minded, vicious jerks whose personalities were mainly composed of things that ended in the letters i-s-t. Racist. Speciesist. Sexist. The only reason she held her tongue was for the sake of the project.

Any conflicts with the soldiers had to go through the chain of command, and the top of the chain here was the biggest asshole of them all. If she said anything to Lieutenant Douglas, he'd make trouble for her, and only her. He'd handpicked his own men for this assignment, which meant they were like-minded and loyal to him.

The only satisfaction she'd had so far was seeing their faces when they'd been informed where they were headed. Douglas had pushed for the tests to be done on one of the corporate-run pleasure planets that were often created near large military bases. Instead, they'd been sent here. Liberty was a relatively undeveloped world with only a single colony. She could observe her subjects in a natural setting while still having the opportunity to introduce them to other sentient species to see if they would choose to create a psychic bond with one of them.

She moved past the building and into open ground. This was the tricky bit.

"*Clear?*" she sent the query to her psy-hawk, Hera.

Once again, the hawk sent her an image of the camp. No one was around. Rin broke into a jog and made for the trees that ringed the camp. The skin on the back of her neck itched, and she felt unsettled and vulnerable. Ten meters to the tree line. Seven. Five. She broke into a sprint for the last few steps, flinging herself into the relative safety and concealment of the woods.

She made it!

Rin pushed deeper into the forest, not stopping until she was sure she was safe from detection. The guards sometimes used infrared goggles to scan the woods, looking for heat sources. So far, they'd only seen a few small animals and one large predator that vanished before they could identify it. The predator sighting was why she'd been ordered not to leave camp without an armed escort.

The problem was, the presence of the soldiers unsettled her subjects and made it impossible for her to record their natural behavior. The psy-hawks actively avoided the soldiers and wanted nothing to do with them.

She felt exactly the same way.

Certain she was in the clear, she signaled Hera to start phase two. A few seconds later, the large, bronze-colored bird sent a visual from her perspective as she flew down from her perch and soared through the window Rin had deliberately left open in the mews earlier that day.

The hawk sent her a series of images as she moved from cage to cage, helping the occupants to free themselves. No one but her knew the animals had taught themselves that little trick. The hawks kept their intelligence carefully hidden from everyone but her.

The IAF had no idea why these birds had been created in the first place, and Rin had done what she could to convince them that their existence was a vanity project by an amoral scientist who developed the creatures for no other reason than because he could.

She suspected the truth was far grimmer and fit perfectly into the military's plans for the hawks—plans she never wanted to come to fruition.

In less than two minutes, all the subjects were free and airborne. Hera sent her a flash of pure joy tinged with mischief at their successful escape. Her bond to the psy-hawk had been a surprise to everyone, including Rin. Before Rin's arrival, the team studying the hawks all experienced moments of telepathic contact with the animals. The contact had all been negative, though, with the hawks using their abilities to warn the humans to stay away.

Rin's connection to Hera was much deeper and flowed both ways. She and the hawk could communicate back and forth via a combination of emotions, images, and words.

When Hera allowed it, Rin could even use their link to tap into the hawk's eyes and ears. Hera's senses were far more acute than her own, and while Hera couldn't understand most human speech, Rin could. Anything Hera saw or heard could be shared with Rin. That's when she realized why the psy-hawks had been created. They were natural spies.

She hadn't shared that information with the military, who claimed ownership of the animals. If they knew their value, Hera and the others would never be freed.

It was another reason she'd worked so hard to convince the oversight committee to allow her to come to Liberty. If the birds chose to bond with other beings while rejecting all military companions, maybe the IAF would lose interest in the project. She just needed to make sure no one figured out their real value until it was too late. Haven colony had been formed to offer a sanctuary to Vardarians looking for a new start and a number of cyborgs that needed a home and a place to heal. She hoped it could be a haven for her hawks, too.

She met the birds in the clearing she'd spotted from the air a few days earlier. The hawks needed daily exercise, and she'd managed to convince Douglas to let her use one of the hover-bikes so she could keep up with them as they flew. He'd insisted on sending two men with her on every flight to "protect her from threats." She knew it was bullshit. He saddled her with guards for the same reason he did everything else, to remind everyone around him that he was in charge.

The clearing was perfect for their needs. Lush grass and flowers came almost to her waist, and she was certain squeakers and other small prey animals would be hidden in the deep grass. Hera had made it clear that the birds wanted time to hunt and enjoy themselves without any soldiers around. Rin had agreed, mostly so she could study the birds without interference and partly to get away from Douglas and his men.

By the time she caught up to the hawks, one of them was already eating something small and furry. The others circled overhead, waiting for their turn to strike.

Rin set up a recording device and hung it on a branch so it had a clear view of the area. Then she leaned against the tree, which grew at the edge of the meadow, and got to work. She used the device to dictate her thoughts as she observed her subjects hunt, play, and interact with each other in the real world instead of the cages where they spent too much of their lives.

This was a huge step for her research. Next, she had to figure out a way to bring them into contact with the citizens of Haven. Since she couldn't leave camp without an escort and the men weren't allowed to enter the colony, she had no idea how the *fraxx* to make that happen.

2

———

As MUCH AS he loved spending time in the outdoors, Axe was more than ready to get home. He wanted a meal cooked by a food dispenser instead of over an open fire, a chance to get good and clean again, and then a good night's sleep in a bed.

"Some battle-hardened cyborg I am. A year living free, and I've gone softer than a peskin's pelt," he muttered to himself. He'd been a scout during the Resource Wars. Living rough for weeks on end, always on the move through enemy territory. Back then, he'd never known the simple pleasures of good food, a warm bed, and a gloriously hot bath. Now he knew what comfort was, he missed it if he was away from home too long.

At least he wasn't as soft as most of his cyborg brethren. They lived in town now, ensconced in homes that seemed like palaces after the brutal conditions they'd endured as test subjects at Reamus Research Station. The corporations' former elite combat troops were now well-fed, educated, and content in ways that worried him. If they ever had to defend their new home, would the younger ones know what to do? Most of them had been created after the war and spent their entire lives as captives until they'd been brought to this place. The only combat they'd seen was against each other, leaving them with scars on their bodies and their psyches.

The Vardarians would fight, of course. Their culture placed a high value on martial skills and training. He attended one of their practice arenas regularly to hone his skills and learn new ones, though he was always careful to pick opponents he knew and trusted. He might not have many friends, but he didn't want to put those he did have in jeopardy by injuring someone.

It was best for everyone if he kept to himself most of the time. His creators had designed him to be a solo operator. He couldn't change who he was or what he'd been made for. It was better for everyone if he was left alone.

That's why he'd signed on with the rangers. They patrolled the wilds around the colony, updated maps, identified wildlife, and safeguarded Haven against threats of all kinds. They'd been the first to document the existence of the *kopaki*—a tunneling predator that could travel through hard dirt and even concrete to get to their prey. The creatures didn't often hunt in the woods around the colony, though. This was ghost cat territory. That was one of the things he liked about the natural world. Each species had its place. If left alone, they stayed in balance with each other.

That thought was chased out of his head by a flash of

a golden-brown *something* darting through the air overhead. He only got a glimpse of it before it was gone, hidden by the canopy of leaves overhead. A single glimpse was enough for him to know that whatever he'd seen didn't belong here.

Axe shifted directions. Instead of heading toward his cabin near the river, he reoriented himself to follow the flight of the unknown animal. This planet was rich with life of all shapes and sizes, but large birds weren't part of the local ecosystem. At least, not that anyone had found so far. Either this creature had literally and figuratively managed to fly under their radar for more than a year, or something odd was going on.

The next time he caught sight of the bird, it wasn't alone. There were two of them now, both a gleaming bronze color with a cream underbelly. They were large animals, with very little size disparity between them. Could it be a parent with a younger bird? Mates? He had no idea. Not yet. He kept following their flight path, aware it would take him straight to an open meadow not far ahead.

The break in the trees was already visible when he heard something else that didn't belong out here—a human voice speaking what sounded like Galactic Common. The tone was low, conversational, and definitely female. He paused to listen, waiting for whoever she was talking with to reply. Once they spoke, he'd have some idea how many were there. Only no one else said a word. Just the one female was talking. The tone and cadence reminded him of some of the digital courses he'd reviewed over the winter. It almost sounded like someone giving a lecture, but who the *fraxx* was she talking to? For that matter, who the hell was she? Only a handful of human women were on the entire planet, and all of them knew better than to wander into the territory he'd claimed for himself.

He didn't like unexpected company, and everyone in the colony knew that.

Axe closed in, moving through the trees with the stealth and patience of a ghost cat on the hunt. He flipped through several visual filters, trying to locate the speaker and anyone else in the area. Eventually, he found her. She was leaning against a tree trunk that obscured most of her body.

He got close enough to make out what she was saying. That's when he realized that what he'd taken for a lecture was more of a running commentary about the animals she observed. She referred to them by numbers, not names.

He growled under his breath, snapped out the extendable staff all rangers carried, and stomped toward her, no longer caring if he made noise. He wanted answers, starting with who the hell she was, why she was here, and who had granted her permission to release a nonnative species of animal in *his* woods?

It took a surprisingly long time for her to react to his imminent arrival. In fact, it took so long he thought she might be ignoring him. Then he remembered how limited human senses were and his annoyance shifted back to concern. Was she out here alone? Didn't she know about the dangerous predators who prowled these woods? Predators like kopaki, ghost cats, and pissed-off cyborgs? She wasn't capable of protecting herself from any of them. Hell, she couldn't even hear him coming. She shouldn't be out here alone. Not unless she had a death wish.

By the time she reacted to his arrival, it was far too late for her to do anything about it.

All she did was move farther into the meadow to put some distance between them and raise her hands in the universal but pointless gesture that translated roughly to "please don't hurt me." Like that ever worked.

She was attractive, in part because she wasn't as small and delicate as most human females. Instead, she was taller than average with a pleasingly rounded figure. Despite her stature, the top of her head didn't quite reach his shoulder.

He cleared the trees and took several steps into the clearing before he stopped to glare at her. "Who are you and why are you here?" he demanded.

To his surprise, the woman glared right back at him, her eyes flashing. "I could ask you the same question. And what's with the stick?"

"It's not a stick. It's a *kes'tarv*, a traditional Vardarian weapon." Then he realized her query had derailed his intended line of questioning. "I'm supposed to be here. I'm Axe and you're on my land." He twirled the staff and pointed one end in her direction. "So I'll ask again. Who are you?"

"I'm Dr. Rin Rey, and I'm here at the invitation of the leadership council of Haven."

He took a moment to remove his backpack and set it down beside him, positioning it so the large axe lashed to the outside was clearly visible. Not a subtle threat, but he wasn't a subtle male.

As he stalled, he considered what she'd said about being invited here.

If that was true, the council was about to get their collective asses kicked, and it still didn't explain why a human was wandering around unaccompanied. "I doubt that," he said.

At that moment, one of the birds he'd followed here shrieked and plummeted out of the sky, coming straight for him.

"Hera, no!" Rin's voice rose in alarm.

Axe dropped to the ground as the bird flew into the space where his head had been a moment before. He sprang back to his feet a second later to see the woman standing with one arm outstretched and the bird perched on her gauntleted forearm.

"We were talking, Hera. He wasn't a threat," Rin scolded the creature.

Axe was almost insulted. No, he *was* insulted. He was most definitely a threat, thank you very much.

After a pause, Rin shook her head. "You can't go around attacking beings because you think they might be dangerous. Besides, if you really thought that, you should have warned me he was here. I think you were showing off."

Another pause. Then Rin frowned at the bird. "I am not helpless! I'm quite capable of protecting myself. And I still think you were showboating."

Either this woman was insane, or she could converse with the animal perched on her arm. If she was mentally unwell, he'd arrange for her to be taken back to Haven. If she wasn't? He wanted to know more about how she managed to communicate with animals. Then they'd circle back to why she was here.

"Are you actually speaking with the bird?" he asked.

She looked up at him as if she'd forgotten he was there. "Huh? Oh. Yes. This is Hera. And I'm sorry she did that to you."

His anger faded at that statement, which surprised him. It usually took longer for him to rein in his temper. It was a fault in his design and the reason why he'd spent most of his life on his own. He suspected his creators had intentionally made him that way, but he'd never know for sure. The techs at Reamus Research Station had deemed him too dangerous and locked him away from the others for most of his imprisonment.

He pushed away thoughts of his past and focused on the present. "And you can actually communicate with her? She speaks to you?"

"Sort of." Rin shrugged. "It's more a mix of images and feelings than actual words most of the time, but we're getting better at it. She seems to understand me when I speak to her. I've theorized that she doesn't understand what I'm saying, but she can sense the intention *behind* the words. Spoken language is an imprecise and messy way of communicating. I'm working to make my own thoughts more precise when I speak with her."

Rin's face lit up as she talked, and Axe found himself paying more attention to *her* than to what she was saying. Her brown eyes gleamed with intelligence and enthusiasm while her dark, wavy hair bounced and swayed in its ponytail as she moved her head and free hand to emphasize her words. He found her intriguing and attractive in a way he hadn't experienced before. Was he experiencing a cognitive malfunction? *Fraxx*, he hoped not.

As Rin spoke, the bird hopped from her arm to her shoulder, its talons gripping the thick leather padding secured by several straps that crossed her chest. It took less than a second to call up the name of the contraption she wore—a pauldron.

"And you brought these animals here to study them? Why?" he asked.

Rin gave him an assessing look, one hand reaching up to stroke Hera's head. "Because Hera and her batch-siblings are military property, and they don't like it. This place is as far away from the IAF's influence as I could manage. I'm grateful your council agreed to allow it."

Her statement included a lot of words Axe didn't like, but the words military, property, and batch-siblings held the majority of his attention. Before he could ask her to expand on her statement, a cascade of images and emotions bombarded his mind as something huge and heavy dropped onto his shoulder.

He was under attack!

3

WHEN RIN IMAGINED BEING able to observe the hawks in a natural environment, this day was exactly what she'd had in mind. What she hadn't envisioned was how their first interaction with the inhabitants of the colony would go. Hell, she wasn't even sure this guy *was* a member of the colony. He was huge, menacing, and rough in every definition of the word. His clothes were patched and worn, his beard was scruffy, and the only clean thing he owned seemed to be the gleaming length of metal he'd called a *kes'tarv*.

He was also the sexiest man she'd ever seen. He had deep green eyes, chiseled features, and a low, rumbling voice she liked far more than she should.

Not that she had time to deal with any of that before things got tense. He growled and barked questions at her... and for a moment she'd thought things were headed to hell in a hyper-driven handcart.

Hera had swooped in to help, risking herself in the process. Axe was a dangerous unknown who could have hurt or even killed the hawk. If that happened, it would be Rin's fault. She wasn't supposed to be out here, even though she'd snuck out expressly to try to achieve the mission's goals despite Douglas's ridiculous rules.

Thankfully, Hera hadn't done more than dive-bomb the new arrival. Now the bird sat safely on her shoulder while she and Axe talked like two civilized beings. Axe seemed calmer now, and he was interested in both Hera and the project. Maybe he'd be willing to interact with the birds or at least introduce her to someone who was.

The thought had barely formed when Subject One streaked out of the sky and attacked Axe.

No! This could not be happening. Rin sent a panicked message to Hera, who chittered at her in mocking tones instead of doing anything about the unfolding disaster.

Then she realized she'd misinterpreted Subject One's actions. The bird wasn't attacking Axe. It was... holy hells and gravity wells. It couldn't be.

Axe spun in place and reached up to grab the hawk, but instead of striking the bird or trying to dislodge it, the big man turned to glare at the psy-hawk latched onto his shoulder.

"Get your talons out of my shoulder and your thoughts out of my *fraxxing* head, bird," Axe snarled.

"You can hear him?" she asked, almost giddy with excitement and relief. This could have gone horribly wrong, but instead she'd gotten her wish. Subject One had bonded with Axe!

Axe grimaced and tapped his temple with one hand. "He's in my head and he won't shut up. It's all a jumble of feelings and images. How do I get him to let go of my shoulder before he does any more damage?"

"Ask him and try visualizing him landing on the ground at your feet when you say it."

Axe grunted. "Sure. Why not? Talk to the bird with daggers on his *fraxxing* feet." He cleared his throat, scowled, and said, "You need to get off my shoulder, Amun. Your talons are tearing me up."

The psy-hawk immediately released Axe's shoulder and fluttered to the ground.

Rin had to bite back an unprofessional squeal of delight. Subject One *had* bonded with Axe. *Fraxx*, was her drone still recording? She hoped so. The little device was programmed to capture images and audio, but she'd left it sitting on a tree in her hurry to put some space between her and the walking mountain of muscled menace when he'd stormed into view.

Axe kept all his attention on Subject One while Rin stared at the growing bloodstains on his shirt. "Um. You're bleeding. I have a small first aid kit with me. Maybe I should look at that?"

He waved her off. "In a minute. I've turned off my pain receptors, and my medi-bots will stop the bleeding on their own. I want to know what the *fraxx* happened and what comes next?"

He could block pain and had nanotech? *Veth.* Axe had to be one of the cyborgs confined to this planet because they were too dangerous and unstable to be allowed to roam the galaxy. Why would Subject One— no, she corrected herself—why would Amun choose to bond with a cybernetic soldier after rejecting so many other members of the military?

She dragged her focus back to the questions Axe had asked. He needed answers, and she was the only one who could provide them.

"The short answer is this: The psy-hawk you call Amun has bonded with you. This is only the second time a bonding has occurred, so the longer answer is complicated and includes a lot of unknowns."

"Only once?" Axe finally looked at her, and she was instantly struck by the uncertainty in his eyes. "I assume the other incident involved you and Hera."

"That's right. Hera and I were the first. They've showed no interest in bonding with anyone they've been introduced to. They don't like the IAF personnel in general, so I assumed they wouldn't bond with anyone in the military." She shrugged, careful not to jostle Hera.

"I'm not military." Axe's declaration was almost a snarl.

"You were a soldier, though." She raised a hand placatingly. "I know it wasn't your choice. Maybe that's why Amun chose you despite your past." She was musing aloud now, working through possibilities. "Or maybe it's because the two of you have so much in common."

"What the *fraxx* could I have common with a *bird?*" Axe demanded and then immediately glanced down at Amun. "No insult intended."

Amun cocked his head and fluffed his wings in a way that somehow conveyed annoyance.

She laughed softly. "I think he's insulted anyway."

"Yeah. Me too."

To her surprise, Axe lowered himself to the ground and sat down beside the psy-hawk. Then he reached out with one huge hand to stroke the bird's back. "I'm going to need some time to wrap my head around this, Amun. I've been on my own for a long time. The only voice I'm used to hearing is mine."

Amun chirped softly and closed the distance between them until he was leaning against Axe's thigh.

"It appears I am forgiven." Axe glanced up at her again. This time, both the uncertainty and the anger were gone. In their place was a look she could only describe as bewildered contentment. Like he was happy but wasn't sure what to make of the feeling.

Without even thinking about it, she sat down beside him and shot him a reassuring smile. "It's a hell of a shock. Isn't it? One minute you're alone in your head and the next you've got someone else in there projecting thoughts and feelings that aren't your own."

He snorted with laughter. "I don't do feelings. They're messy and lead to bad decisions."

"Spoken like a typical guy." *Fraxx.* Had she said that aloud? What a time for her filters to fail. She needed to be at her professional best. After all, this was exactly what she'd hoped for when she'd come to Haven, and she wanted to document everything that happened from now until she had to leave.

Axe shot her a wry look, somewhere between amused and insulted. "I'm not typical and I'm not a guy. I'm a cyborg."

"I figured that out." She raised a hand and ticked off each point she made on her fingers. "You have medi-bots. You said you turned off your pain receptors. Oh, yes, and you're *fraxxing* huge. I swear I've seen Torskis smaller than you."

His smile widened, transforming the hard planes of his face into a portrait of breathtaking male beauty. "You're exaggerating. The only members of that species smaller than me are juveniles."

Several important parts of her brain shorted out when he smiled, and she had to struggle to form her next words. "You're right, but my statement is still technically true."

"Now you sound like a corporate executive." His light, teasing tone indicated he was joking, but the words still hit her like a slap to the face.

"Now *I'm* insulted. I'm not affiliated with any of the corporations. I do freelance work for them from time to time, but that's it. I won't compromise my integrity for a paycheck."

His eyes widened and Amun made a show of pecking his leg in disapproval while Hera hopped to the ground and positioned herself so she could glare at the cyborg.

"Sorry. I didn't mean to offend you." He scowled and raked a hand through his long hair. "I mentioned I'm often alone already. Too much time solo and my social skills get rusty."

"It's fine. I just wanted to make it clear I'm not on any corporation's payroll. Not that most of them would have much use for an ornithologist."

"I don't imagine many of them care much about birds," he agreed. "But I would have said the same thing about the IAF, yet here you are."

Rin paused for a moment to collect her thoughts and confirm that nothing she was about to reveal was classified. Douglas would have her head if she gave away military secrets. When she spoke, she made sure her voice was low enough the recording drone wouldn't catch what she said. "I assume you know where the corporations acquired the original genetic material used to create the cyborgs?"

He nodded and dropped his volume to match hers. "They stole it from the Vault of the Fallen. I gather that's some kind of genetic vault the Interstellar Armed Forces has hidden away on a secret base somewhere."

Rin confirmed his statement with a silent nod that would give her some wiggle room if she was asked what she'd revealed about Victor Base and the secrets hidden inside its walls.

"Recently the IAF reviewed a number of projects and materials from that location and discovered that one of the former scientists had been running a project off the books." She gestured to Hera and Amun and then to the others still circling overhead. "The notes are encrypted, and so far the IAF hasn't been able to read them. All they had to go on were the eight fertilized eggs stored in a cryo-tube."

Axe curled his lip in disgust. "Let me guess. They decided the best way to figure out the experiment was to hatch the eggs and see what came out?"

"Uh. Yeah. Not the way I'd have done it, but they didn't bring me on board until later. The subjects were all full-fledged adults by then, and Hera bonded with me immediately. Until then, they had no idea that was one of their abilities."

"They're *fraxxing* lucky Amun and his kin weren't dragons or something equally dangerous."

Amun chirped at him before lifting one foot to flex his talons and then looking pointedly at Axe's bloody shirt.

"Point taken." Axe grinned at the hawk. "You're plenty dangerous, bird."

Veth. She was in trouble. He wasn't even looking at her and his smile still melted the edges of her brain and made her pulse trip like a hammer. Rin reminded herself that she needed to stay focused and professional. Axe might be the hottest man she'd ever met, but he was now part of her project, and that meant he was off limits.

She was the hawks' best chance at a good life—one free from the IAF and its desire to weaponize the animals. She couldn't do anything to jeopardize the study, and that included flirting with the hot and grumpy cyborg.

4

This day kept surprising him. All he wanted to do was get home, enjoy a hot shower, eat a good meal, and then get back to work on a number of projects he needed to finish. His customers knew he worked on his own schedule, but he couldn't start anything new until he completed a few of the larger projects to make room.

Now he had Amun in his head and a distractingly lovely human woman seated beside him, offering to check on his wounded shoulder and explaining that he now shared some kind of psychic link to a *fraxxing* bird. Both situations demanded his attention, and he had no idea which one to deal with first.

Amun sent him a brief pulse of amusement accompanied by an image of Rin.

Great. Now the bird was giving him advice. Worse, he was inclined to take it. If Amun wanted his attention, he would let him know. That meant his focus should be on Rin, the temptingly pretty scientist who didn't consider him a threat. Not that he was still stung about that or anything.

"Speaking of Amun being dangerous, I'd still like to take a look at you," Rin said. Then her eyes widened and her cheeks heated. "I, uh, I mean, I should look at your injured shoulder. I feel responsible for what happened."

Damn, she was even prettier when she got flustered. It made her look sweet and vulnerable—two things he never imagined would appeal to him in a female. Until now.

He meant to tell her he'd be fine. What came out instead was, "It wasn't your fault. Amun surprised us both. If you need to see for yourself, though. I won't argue."

"*Are you doing this?*" He sent the thought to Amun without saying it aloud. Communicating this way was a lot like speaking to his fellow cyborgs on their internal comm channels. If Amun didn't need to hear his words to understand him, it would be easier, and no one would wonder why he'd started talking to himself.

Amun sent back a thought Axe interpreted as a negative. If the bird wasn't messing with him, he'd either lost his mind or Rin was affecting him in ways he didn't want to contemplate.

"I'd feel better if I knew you were healing up," Rin said as she got to her feet.

He pulled his shirt over his head before his brain had time to process what was happening. It was a good thing he'd stopped to bathe and swim in the river this morning or even Rin's unenhanced senses would have suffered.

Rin crouched down behind him and swore. "Holy

fraxx. He really made a mess of your shoulder. I'll bring you a pauldron and a gauntlet so this doesn't happen again."

"I'd appreciate that." He doubted she'd have a glove that would fit him, but he had friends who could copy the design and produce something in his size.

The gentle touch of her hands on his back surprised him. He hadn't expected the contact at all, never mind the soft and careful way she stroked his skin.

"You have so many scars," she murmured. "No wonder you're not concerned about your new injury."

"I was a scout during the Resource Wars. I spent most of that of time alone in enemy territory, and I got shot at a lot." He shrugged. "My medi-bots kept me alive and combat capable. The scars are just reminders of the wounds that didn't kill me."

She ran her fingertips over his scars, careful not to touch the still-healing wounds on his shoulder. The touch triggered a wave of goose bumps up his spine as his cock surged to life.

"Judging by all of these, you must be immortal."

"I'm a cyborg," he reminded her. "We're designed to be hard to kill." That was the point of their entire existence. They were created to be the perfect soldiers—human enough to circumvent the laws against waging wars with machines but enhanced and altered enough to be bigger, stronger, faster, and more obedient. They were meant to be programmed to kill without remorse and never question orders. Only the corporations screwed up. Given time, the cyborgs overcame their programming and became fully self-aware. Then, they rose up and demanded their freedom. Most were freed. Some, like him, were captured and experimented on to see what went wrong.

"I should get my kit and clean up these wounds. I know the medi-bots can handle it, but there's a lot of blood. When it dries, it's going to itch."

Axe was shocked into silence again. She worried he'd be uncomfortable? No one ever worried about his comfort. This woman kept surprising him, and he didn't like that she somehow managed to make him feel vulnerable and off-balance.

Amun and Hera shrieked a warning and took to the air a second later. His hawk filled his head with a sense of danger accompanied by an image of an angry human male dressed in military garb.

Axe shot to his feet and pulled Rin behind him as he scanned the woods for whoever Amun had warned him about.

"Dammit. They found me," Rin muttered and tried to move in front of him. "Douglas! I know you're out there. Show yourself."

Axe dragged her back behind him. "Who is Douglas?" he demanded.

"Lieutenant Douglas is in charge of this project. Well, the military aspects of it, anyway."

Axe wanted to roar in frustration. The council had allowed the IAF to come to Haven? Why hadn't anyone told him? "I thought you said Haven was as far away from the military as you could manage? How can that be if they're *here*?"

"It's just Douglas and a small squad put together for

this mission. None of them are allowed near the subjects. They're prohibited from entering Haven, too. The IAF doesn't want their highly trained assets randomly bonding to alien females, and the leadership council preferred the soldiers stay out of town and away from their citizens."

A rustle in the trees ended their conversation. Axe turned toward the noise and scanned the forest for heat signatures. He spotted seven of them, all human.

"Dr Rey. Step away from the hostile immediately," a voice commanded.

"For the love of gravity, Douglas. He's not a hostile. He lives here! And as of ten minutes ago, he's part of the project."

"The hell he is! Get away from the hostile now. Or did you miss the fact he's a cyborg?"

Axe drew his *kes'tarv* and held it at his side without extending it. If they attacked him, he had a surprise waiting. The staff he carried was modified and had a blaster built into one end.

Rin ignored the lieutenant's orders and Axe's wishes by deliberately placing herself between him and the area where the soldiers hid.

"Hera can see them and can feed me images of where they are and what they're doing. None of them have their weapons raised except for Douglas, and he won't shoot at me," she whispered.

Axe hissed his next words through gritted teeth. "I don't need your protection. I should be protecting *you*."

She glanced over her shoulder at him and gave him a brief but sassy smile. "It can be your turn next time."

He braced for the surge of anger that always rose when someone pushed him this far, but it never came. He was annoyed and concerned for Rin's safety, but that was all.

Amun sent a gentle pulse of calm, and this time, he sensed it. The bird was helping him control his anger, and it worked! Axe sent a message of gratitude back, but he couldn't dwell on what had happened or what it meant. He had immediate issues to deal with. Starting with Rin. The curvy little scientist had more courage than common sense, and it occurred to him that someway, somehow, Rin would be the death of him. It would probably involve a firefight or a fatal case of frustration.

Douglas called out again, "Dammit, Dr. Rey. It's bad enough you snuck out without permission or a protective detail. Now you're making it impossible for us to do our job, which is to protect you and the project."

The underbrush rustled again, and this time the lieutenant stepped into view. He looked like every other officer Axe had seen—clean cut, an arrogant expression, and wearing brightly polished boots that had never seen a battlefield. He hated him on sight.

Rin folded her arms and stood her ground. "I don't need your permission to do *my* job, Lieutenant. Your rules have made it almost impossible for me to complete the goals of this project. I can prove it, too. Today was the first time I went out alone, and I've already recorded a bonding between Subject One and this man."

"What?" Douglas sounded equally exasperated and incredulous. "That's not possible. The birds have refused to bond with anyone linked to the military! He's a *cyborg*.

One of the most dangerous weapons in the galaxy. There's no way I'm going to allow one of *them* to be part of this project."

Axe decided it was time to join the conversation. "It's not your call to make. Amun chose to bond with me. Dr. Rey has confirmed that already. Like it or not, Amun and I are part of this now. And for the record, I'm not a weapon. I'm a living being whose rights are recognized by all known governments and species."

He heard muttering and grumbles from the other soldiers, but none of them spoke in more than hushed whispers. Rin wouldn't get any help from them, even though they sounded more resigned than concerned. Douglas was the problem here.

"I don't like it and I won't believe it until I've seen solid proof. Dr. Rey, you and your subjects need to return to camp. Now. Once there, you and I will discuss this matter further." Douglas glared at Axe. "You are free to go, cyborg."

"I'm also free to stay. As Rin stated, I'm a citizen of Haven." Axe pointed to the ground at his feet. "In fact, you are currently standing on *my* land. Check with the leadership council if you need confirmation, but this is private property. Rin has my permission to be here. You don't. I suggest you leave. Rin can leave or stay as she chooses." He held out his arm and called to Amun.

"Try not to rip up my arm, bird."

The hawk replied with a quick mental tap that felt like an acknowledgment. A few seconds later, Amun dove out of the sky and made straight for him. The hawk back-winged at the last minute, extended his talons, and wrapped them carefully around Axe's forearm without so much as a scratch.

"Nicely done, Amun," he said loudly enough for Douglas to hear him.

The lieutenant's face contorted into something that conveyed either acute frustration or an unexpected bowel movement.

The hawk looked smug and flapped his wings once before settling again.

"Show-off," Rin whispered to the hawk.

"That is IAF property. I demand you return the subject at once," Douglas snapped out the order as if he expected to be obeyed.

That wasn't happening.

"No. Subject One *was* IAF property. Amun belongs with me now." Axe chose his words with care. He'd been a possession himself and would never claim ownership over an intelligent being like Amun, even if the bird was going to be a pain in his ass.

Douglas stiffened and opened his mouth to argue, but Rin cut him off. "Check the mission briefing, Lieutenant. Once bonded, the psy-hawks must stay with their chosen partner. Hera explained it, and we did enough testing to confirm it's true. Amun stays with Axe."

"Dr. Rey. The IAF did not bring these creatures here so you could give them away to random strangers."

"Actually, that's exactly what I hoped would happen. We have confirmation that the bonding between Hera and me wasn't a one-off event. That was one of the primary goals. Leadership understood that meant some of the subjects may not return."

"Like I said. Amun stays with me. Rin is, of course, welcome to visit to observe and take notes any time she likes." Axe decided it was time to throw a *kopaki* into the proverbial henhouse and added, "And she is welcome to bring the remaining subjects with her when she visits."

It wasn't until after he spoke that he realized what he'd done. He'd just offered an open invitation to Rin and her flock of featherheads to visit anytime they wanted.

Most of the *fraxxing* colony didn't even know where he lived, and he liked it that way. What the hell was happening?

One look at the curvy woman staring down an IAF officer and he had his answer. *Rin* happened to him. He'd approached her because he thought she might be a threat. Turns out he'd been right. She was dangerous to his sanity, and if he wasn't careful, she could be a threat to the solitary but comfortable life he was building out here.

Fraxx.

5

———

Rin wanted to shout for joy and possibly do a victory dance, but she stayed still and calm despite what had just happened. Axe's offer was the perfect solution to her problems. Douglas and his men couldn't follow her onto the cyborg's land, so she'd be free to observe both the psy-hawks and Axe's interactions with Amun without interference.

The fact she'd also get to spend more time alone with him was totally irrelevant. He was off limits despite the fact her fingers still tingled from touching him, and she kept revisiting the memory of what he looked like with his shirt off. She'd never seen a man with that much muscle...or that many scars. Cyborg or not, he must be tough as hull plating to survive so many injuries.

Douglas looked like he was going to choke on his own tongue, but he backed down with a sullen nod. "I will contact the council to discuss this... turn of events. Dr. Rey, you will come with us." He snapped his fingers and pointed to the ground in front of him. "Immediately."

She raised her chin and tried to ignore the insult. She already knew Douglas's opinion of her, but this was a new low. She wasn't his pet to be summoned with a snap of his fingers, dammit. Still, she elected to take the higher orbit.

Axe didn't. He snarled under his breath, moved around her, and took several steps toward Douglas. The asshole lieutenant raised his weapon and stood firm.

Veth. If one of them didn't back down, someone was going to get hurt. Probably both of them, since Douglas would likely shoot first, piss Axe off, and then get the beating of his life. As much as she disliked Douglas, if he was injured, it would put the whole project at risk of being canceled. She couldn't let that happen.

Acting on instinct, she moved to Axe's side and took hold of his hand. He started at her touch and dropped his gaze to glare at her, but she just squeezed his fingers and smiled. "It's okay, Axe," she said in a tone too low for Douglas to hear. "He's an asshole who uses his rank to make himself feel important. The more you react, the better he feels about whatever he's overcompensating for. Ignoring him is the fastest way to piss him off."

"Or I could just tear his head off and give it to Amun to play with." His words were dark, but his eyes glinted with amusement and a ghost of a smile played around his mouth.

"Let's call that Plan B."

Amun chirped at her and she gave him a pat on the head as he perched on Axe's arm. "He'll need fresh water and a place to sleep out of the weather. They were born in captivity and haven't had time to adapt to a more natural life. He can hunt for himself if he's hungry, and I'll bring you more supplies tomorrow."

Axe's smile vanished. "You're leaving? With *him?*" Disdain dripped from the end of his question.

"If I don't go with him, he'll twist everything that happened today. He'll make sure his report is tailored to fit his preferred narrative. I should be there when he speaks to the local leadership, too. He's likely to try to blame everything on you."

Axe glanced over at Douglas, who looked increasingly impatient, and then back at her. "He's welcome to try and blame me. The council will probably be stunned he's still alive and has all his teeth when they hear he was on my land without permission. I'm more worried about you."

That simple statement turned her brain to mush for a moment. This massive and dangerous man, one designed from the DNA up to be a killer, wanted to protect her. At that second, she saw him in a new light. No wonder Amun had bonded with Axe. They were both products of someone's experiments, created for a purpose they rejected, with the same desire to exist in peace.

She squeezed his fingers even harder and then released him. "I'll be okay. I promise. He's a bully, but he's ambitious enough not to cross a line that could tarnish his reputation."

"If he comes anywhere near that line, you will tell me." It wasn't a question but a statement. "You can ask anyone on the council for my contact information. Tell them you have my permission, but if they give it to anyone else, I will not be pleased."

She laughed. "I'll do that if you stop bossing me around. I can take care of myself. I need you to promise you'll take care of Amun."

He bowed his head and met her gaze. "You have my word. He'll have everything he needs to be free and happy."

They stared at each other for a few more seconds with both of them breaking eye contact at the same moment.

"I'll see you tomorrow. We can sort out the details when you contact me," he said.

"See you both tomorrow. Take care of each other." She smiled at both the man and the psy-hawk and then turned toward Douglas. His scowling countenance confirmed what she already knew. It would be a long walk home.

"... and then I find you far from camp, cozied up with a half-naked cyborg! Do I have to remind you how dangerous those things are? Especially to a woman on her own? The corporations messed with their hormones to make them even more aggressive. You were taking more than your life into your hands just being close to it."

Douglas hadn't stopped ranting since they'd left the meadow. Rin had tuned him out for the most part, but his latest accusation couldn't be left uncontested.

"Lieutenant Douglas, you know full well I was checking on Axe's injured shoulder. You, of all people, should be aware that the psy-hawks can do significant damage with their talons." He'd been attacked by the subjects several times since he'd joined the project. He'd finally learned not to poke and prod at them like they were objects instead of living creatures.

"Cyborgs heal at an accelerated rate. He didn't need your assistance. If I hadn't arrived when I did..." He trailed off, his implications clear. He wanted her to thank him for saving her from some dire fate he'd dreamed up. The man's ego was out of control.

"I don't believe I was in any danger. If he'd been a threat, Amun would not have bonded with him. As for today's events, I've already given you an explanation for everything that occurred. Be assured I will submit an update once I'm back at camp. I'm certain the higher ups will be pleased to hear that the project is progressing."

"I wouldn't call today's outcome progress. You gave away one of the rarest animals in the galaxy to a cybernetic psychopath. You do realize that once our time here is over, you'll likely never be allowed to return?" Douglas shot her a look of pure vitriol laced with exasperation. "This has to be what the local leadership hoped for when they agreed to let us come here. You've played right into their plans."

Douglas was throwing blame around in hopes it stuck to someone else, which was ridiculous.

"I don't understand your point. There was always a risk that some, or even all, of the subjects might bond and stay on the planet. That's why a male and female psy-hawk were left in the IAF's care," she pointed out gently.

He knew that already. Hell, he'd been the one to tell her about the last-minute change in plans. She assumed she wasn't told until after they'd left orbit because the brass knew she'd be angry and wanted to avoid a confrontation. It worked, too. There was no point in arguing once they were in transit. She'd let the matter go because any kind of protest was pointless and would only irritate the ones paying her salary.

"Right. Of course." He waved away her point like it was an annoying bug. "But still, every one of the subjects is a valuable asset."

Rin arranged her features into the calmest expression she could manage before replying. Once the lieutenant was agitated, it was pointless to try and argue or protest, so she simply moved on to her next point.

"I'm sure the local leadership wouldn't refuse my request to return at some future point, especially if it benefited Axe and Amun. But even if I'm not allowed back, it wouldn't impact you in any way. This mission is only set to last another two weeks, Lieutenant. After that, I won't be your responsibility anymore."

"That's the point, Dr. Rey. Until then, you and these subjects are my responsibility. What happened today cannot happen again. Do you understand?"

She gave a brief nod, despite the fact she didn't see the point he was trying to make. Still, if she appeared agreeable, maybe he'd end this conversation and let her get back to work.

No such luck.

He fixed her with a stern gaze. "I need you to confirm that you understand my directives and will obey them for the safety of you and the project."

"I understand that you are responsible for the safety

of everyone involved in this project, Lieutenant Douglas." She nearly added that it wasn't her intention to put herself or the subjects in danger, but it would only ramp up his anger again. Plus, it wasn't entirely true. She *had* snuck out of camp without her escort. The thing was, Douglas refused to see that the hawks were all the protection she needed.

"Which is why I am monitoring your location." His expression turned dark and predatory for a brief but disturbing moment. "Or did you think we found you so quickly out of pure luck?"

The son of a bitch was tracking her. She managed to rein in her anger but not her expression, which was all he needed to know he'd scored a direct hit. "You can't do that. It's a violation of my rights."

"I can do that. Didn't you read the mission briefing?" He threw her earlier words back at her. "For the duration of this project, your personal rights are secondary to the goals of the mission. That includes the safety of you and the subjects."

And since he was in charge of security, he could, and obviously would, use that clause to control her. His interpretation was twisted to suit his needs, of course. But he was the highest-ranking officer on the planet. Hell, he was the only officer in the whole damned system. *Fraxx.*

She allowed her shoulders to slump in apparent defeat and bowed her head. "I see."

Douglas wasn't done gloating. "I don't care if you see it," he hissed at her. "I want to know if you understand what I said and what it means."

She kept her head down because she wasn't confident

she could hide her anger if she looked at him right now. "I understand perfectly, Lieutenant Douglas."

"Good. Now, I need you to *understand* one more thing, Dr. Rey. You will never release all the subjects from their cages at once again without my permission."

"Understood." This time, she kept her head down to hide her smile. Douglas still didn't realize that the birds were intelligent enough to free each other. So long as one of them was out of their cage, all of them could be released.

Next, she would teach them how to open the cages from the inside. Douglas might have control of her for now... but she'd never let him have full control over the animals in her care.

6

Axe shadowed the soldiers escorting Rin until they left his property. Amun assisted him by flying overhead and feeding him images of the group as they moved through the trees. Nothing either he or Amun saw impressed him. The soldiers looked like they were on a nature hike instead of a military excursion. Their formation was sloppy and their attitude one of distracted boredom.

Douglas either didn't notice or didn't care what his men did. His attention was focused on Rin, and from what Axe heard and saw, the arrogant ass was ranting and blaming Rin for everything. He was the *fraxxing* officer in charge. If a civilian scientist could slip out of camp unseen with a half-dozen birds in tow, the problem wasn't Rin.

Obviously, this barrel of monkeys couldn't be trusted with Rin's safety.

"If you want something done right, do it yourself," he muttered to himself and then remembered he had a partner now. One who could fly.

"*Make sure they get back to camp safely,*" he sent to Amun.

The bird responded with a blast of images and fragmented thoughts Axe couldn't translate. "*Repeat that but slower.*"

Apparently, the bird understood snark because this time the communication was painfully slow. He received two images of the retreating group from slightly different perspectives and a sense of plurality.

"*Gotcha. You don't need to follow them yourself because you're linked to the rest of the subjects.*" He remembered what Rin had said about focusing on intent when communicating with the birds and tried to make his thoughts clear.

Amun sent him a pulse of acknowledgment and approval.

"Smart ass bird," he grumbled to himself, more amused than annoyed. He watched until Rin and the others faded from sight before turning toward his cabin. Food and a hot shower would have to wait until Amun was settled.

Where the hell would he put the hawk? In the house? Unlikely. In the chicken coop? Hell *fraxxing* no. That was a recipe for disaster.

"*Amun?*" he sent to his new companion. "*How do you feel about the smell of sawdust and wood?*"

His first sight of home always gave him a warm feeling he'd never known until Haven. His friends and fellow rangers, Wreckage and Ruin, had kept an eye on the place while he'd been gone. That mostly meant they'd watered his small garden and taken care of his chickens. They knew better than to go inside his house.

Amun flew down to land on the roof of the chicken coop. His arrival sent the small flock squawking in alarm as they bolted for shelter.

"*Food?*" the bird sent.

"*Not your food. My food. You protect?*"

The hawk sent a flash of amusement and something Axe translated as, "*I protect stupid food birds.*"

"Thanks," he said aloud. He unlocked the door and checked to ensure the chickens had food and water before securing the coop again. The local predators would be happy to devour his entire flock if given half a chance. Because of that, his birds lived in the chicken version of a high-security prison with heavy locks, unbreachable fences, and a metal plate buried beneath the entire structure.

"I live there." He pointed to his cabin, a two-story building that had taken him months to build because he'd done it all himself. Well, almost all. He'd borrowed one of the Vardarian construction machines to create the basic structure. The rest had been a labor of love.

"I think you'll be comfortable in my workshop. It's large, warm, dry, and I can leave the doors open so you can come and go as you please. Later, we'll figured out something for the winter months."

Amun chirped and took to the air. He crossed the clearing in a few seconds and landed just outside the shop. He immediately sent an image of the inside of the space to Axe, accompanied by a sense of inquisition.

Axe explained as he caught up. "This is where I work. I chop down trees and bring the wood here to turn it into other things. Furniture mostly. Some art pieces and sculptures. I trade or sell them and use the income to buy what I need." He didn't know how much of that Amun would understand, but he explained it all, anyway.

"I used to be a soldier. But when I was sent here I wanted to do anything but fight. I helped clear the land for the colony. That's when I learned how to fell trees and, well, how to be a sort of lumberjack. Sometimes I do patrols in the woods, too. You can come with me if you like."

The hawk bobbed his head in what Axe swore was a nod and hopped inside. Axe stopped to flip on the lights and then followed Amun into his favorite place in the galaxy.

The scent of sawdust and wood hung in the air, and everywhere he looked were things he'd created. Someone on his design team had included a few basic skills in his programming. Not only could he cook, but his skill set also included a decent understanding of wood carving. He'd whittled all sorts of small objects during his scouting years. He'd never been allowed to keep any of them, though. Cyborgs weren't permitted to have possessions since they were considered to *be* possessions.

That wasn't true anymore. Now he was free to create and keep anything he wanted. Every tree he used was carefully selected and felled with the axe he always carried with him. He'd chopped down several trees on his last patrol. He'd have to go out and retrieve them soon. Overhangs on both sides of the workshop provided plenty of space to set out raw logs and other pieces to dry before they were used. Axe breathed in deeply, letting the scent settle deep in his lungs. A sense of calm washed over him, smoothing away the jagged edges of his personality. At least for the moment.

By that time, Amun had already flown up into the rafters and chosen a perch.

"Will this work for you?" he asked the bird.

Amun sent him a strong pulse of approval and pleasure.

Well, that was easy. It only took a few minutes to find a suitable container and fill it with fresh water. Once that was done, he glanced up at Amun. "I'm going inside. You're welcome to come in, too. But if you make a mess of my home, I won't be happy."

Amun issued a strident chirp accompanied by a sense of displeasure.

Axe held up a hand. "Don't get your feathers in a twist. I wasn't trying to insult you. I would say the same thing to anyone I invited into my home." Not that he'd had any visitors. His fellow rangers all had at least a vague idea of where he lived, but very few actually visited, and none had ever been inside. Most of them enjoyed their solitude as much as he did.

That thought led him to consider Wreckage and Ruin's situation. They'd recently fallen in love with a human woman. As a result, they were now more involved with the colony on a day-to-day basis, and that wasn't the only difference. Jade had altered the trajectory of their entire lives. At the time, he'd thought they were crazy. Today? He wasn't so sure. Amun had literally dropped into his life from the clear blue sky, and despite the invasiveness of their psychic bond, he was already adjusting to life with an unexpected companion. He'd even issued Rin an open invitation to visit him for *fraxx's* sake. That had to be Amun's doing.

Thoughts of Rin stayed with him while he stripped naked and dropped his clothes into the laundry chute for the household bots to deal with. He might live away from the colony, but that didn't mean he hadn't found ways to include some of the perks of modern living into his home. Why do laundry or clean the house when bots were capable of doing the same task faster and more efficiently?

Something crashed to the floor on the lower level. The second floor was a loft that overlooked the common room below, so he could tell Amun was in the kitchen. "I told you not to wreck my house, bird!"

Amun flew up to his level and landed on the railing with remarkable grace considering he had one of the local rodents in one talon. The hawk gave him a haughty look and held out his dead prize.

"That was in the kitchen?" The damned squeakers kept finding new ways into his house.

Amun bobbed his head in what he now thought of as a nod.

"Thanks. You're welcome to kill anything else that wanders into the house without permission."

The bird chirped sharply and raised his claw as if he was about to chow down. "Hold up. Catching them is fine. Eating them in the house is a nonstarter. I'm sure my cleaning bots don't have a remove blood and viscera setting. Eat outside, and then you're welcome to come back in. Meanwhile, I am going to have a shower. Do not disturb me on pain of... something."

The bird flew off with the rodent, and Axe got a brief flash of amusement followed by an image of Rin approaching a standard military habi-pod. She'd made it back to camp. *Good.*

Next time he'd walk back with her. Having seen the incompetent idiots assigned to protect her, he'd have to take over that job. If he didn't, the pretty little scientist was likely to get eaten by one of the local predators... or claimed by a couple of Vardarian males.

That wasn't going to happen. Not on his watch. He needed her help to understand his newly bonded companion. Until he had all the answers he needed, she wasn't going anywhere.

He turned on the hot water and stepped under the stream as soon as it was warm. First, he'd been a scout and then a prisoner. These days he was both a ranger and a craftsman. As of now, he had a new title to add to his nonexistent résumé. *Protector.*

7

SINCE HER ACCIDENTAL encounter with Axe the other day, Rin felt like everything had finally fallen into place. Her subjects enjoyed their extended time away from the camp and Douglas's men, and her observations of the bonding between Axe and Amun expanded her understanding of the process. Their conversations helped her see things from another angle and generated almost as many questions as it did answers, but it was *progress*.

Douglas continued to be difficult, but even his sour moods and sharp comments didn't hit her the way they had before. She told herself it was because the project was finally producing results, but that was only partially true. She enjoyed Axe's company so much it was affecting her mood even when they were apart. It wasn't just physical attraction, either. He had a dry wit, a sharp mind, and a softer side that was apparent every time she watched him interact with Amun.

Each morning she woke up eager to see him again, and every night she saw him again in her dreams. Their daytime sessions were all logged and recorded, but her dreams… Just the thought of what she'd imagined doing with Axe made her ache for things that could never happen.

"He's off limits," she reminded herself as she made her way across the camp. "Not to mention he's light years out of your league."

Axe stepped into view a few seconds later, and all her good intentions went flying out the airlock again. Her breath hitched in her lungs and her heart did a fluttery-jump thing in her chest just at the sight of him.

Hera sent her a brief pulse of happiness accompanied by an image of the cyborg through the hawk's vastly superior eyes. *Veth*, he was breathtaking. He looked as if he could be an avatar of an ancient god of nature or a warrior from another time. Today, his hair was tied back in a low ponytail. He'd trimmed his beard and tidied himself since their first meeting, though his fashion choices hadn't changed. Dark shirts, dark pants, heavy boots, and the expandable staff he called a *kes'tarv* at his hip.

It didn't matter what he wore. He looked incredible. *See? Hundreds of light years out of your league*, she reminded herself.

Two soldiers joined her as she left the camp and made her way to where Axe stood waiting.

Douglas's men accompanied her on each of these trips to the meadow where she'd first met the big cyborg. They were her official security detail, but that hadn't stopped Axe from meeting her at the edge of the forest just a few hundred meters from camp.

When she asked about it, he stated the soldiers were more likely to get her killed than protect her, so he'd see to her safety himself.

Of course, he'd said this while the men were within earshot. Douglas had not been pleased, but he could do nothing about it. Axe was a civilian, and they were guests here.

"Good morning," she called out to Axe.

"Morning." He flashed her a brief but warm smile before letting his expression go blank again. He never spoke or showed much emotion until they were alone. Not that he transformed into mister smiles-and-sunshine when they were alone, but he did loosen up somewhat.

"How's Amun today?" she asked.

Axe rolled his eyes and moved in close to her before speaking in low tones the others wouldn't hear. "The bird is full of attitude. This morning he left a freshly killed *tumpa* on my doorstep. When I asked why, he implied I wasn't much of a hunter, and he thought I needed some help."

Rin couldn't help it. She burst out laughing. "Harsh words."

"It's *fraxxing* insulting. He hasn't even seen me hunt yet."

"That's probably why he thinks you need help. His kind hunt at least once a day."

"So you're saying I need to explain to him what a cooling unit is and why I don't need to get fresh meat every day? Great. I'll toss his feathery ass inside it tonight and he can discover what beings with opposable thumbs instead of wings can accomplish."

The relationship between Axe and Amun was very different from the one she had with Hera. She suspected it had to do with the hawks' psychic abilities. From what little data she had, either the birds adapted their personality to match their companions, or they choose companions who were already compatible. She'd need more information before she could confirm anything.

She pursed her lips and pretended to consider his threat. "If you do that, he'll probably eat everything in the cooler."

"Good point. He can find his own dinner." Axe glanced up at the sky. She couldn't see the birds from this distance, but the cyborg could. She'd had no idea how many enhancements the corporations had made to their former creations until she'd met Axe. He hadn't said much, but what little she learned helped her understand why he didn't think of himself as human anymore.

The group of them walked through the woods to the boundary Axe had pointed out to them the first morning.

"I'll take it from here, boys," he told the two men acting as her security detail.

"See you at the usual time," she added. The two would return to camp for a few hours before returning to collect her for the midday meal.

It was one of Lt. Douglas's petty new rules. She wasn't supposed to leave the area around the meadow. She had to return to camp to eat and transfer all the new recordings and notes. Most annoying, he hadn't backed down from his edict that she couldn't bring all the hawks with her on any excursion for "security reasons." Hera could accompany her, but two of the remaining subjects had to stay behind.

This morning she had Subjects Two and Five with her. After lunch, she'd bring out Four and Six. It was the best solution she could come up with.

Once they were alone, Axe warmed up quickly. He pointed out various animals that lived in the woods and instructed her on potential dangers.

Yesterday, he'd shown her a bark spider. After that, she'd been tempted to run back to camp and hide in her habi-pod. The flattened, plate-sized nightmare fodder had a horrifying number of legs and fangs filled with venom. As a bonus, the damned things were perfectly camouflaged to match the bark of the trees they lived on while waiting to ambush prey... or anything they thought might be edible. Apparently, that included humans.

After that discovery, she kept her hands at her sides and made a concerted effort not to walk too close to anything that could house one of the creatures.

Thoughts of the local wildlife inevitably led her back to her favorite topic—the psy-hawks.

"It's interesting this area has no winged predators. It's an ideal location for the hawks because there's no competition," she mused.

Hera sent her a quick reminder that *she* was a winged predator and she was here, so that wasn't true anymore.

"I know, Hera. But we're not staying. Remember?" She continued her habit of talking out loud to her companion. Axe understood and seemed to enjoy hearing her side of the conversation.

The hawk sent her a flash of disappointment and sorrow followed by an image of Amun flying nearby.

"Everything okay?" Axe asked. "You stopped smiling."

"I did?" Part of her was surprised he noticed. The rest of her was still caught up in the emotions Hera had sent. She felt the same way as her companion. Leaving Amun here alone didn't sit well with her. She didn't like the thought of never seeing Axe again, either. But that was a different issue.

"*Not different. Same. Same.*" Hera's thoughts came through with surprising clarity and the feelings that accompanied the message were... romantic? At least that's how she interpreted them. For the love of gravity, was her bird falling for Amun the same way she was falling for Axe?

Rin slammed the brakes hard on that entire line of thinking.

"What stole your smile?" Axe asked in a surprisingly soft tone that launched a flurry of butterflies in her stomach.

"Hera." She tapped her temple. "She told me she'll be sad when we leave. I think she'll miss this place and Amun."

They were still a few minutes away from the meadow, but Axe stopped walking and turned to look at her. "What about you? Will you miss this place?"

They stood so close together she had to crane her neck to look at him properly. The smart thing to do was obvious—make some vague comment about Haven being a beautiful place she'd remember forever.

She didn't do the smart thing. Her brain wasn't involved in her next words at all. They came from out of nowhere and shoved her off a proverbial cliff. "I will. This planet is still wild and mostly untouched. There's so much I could learn here. But that's not what I'll miss the most."

It seemed as if the entire forest held its collective breath as they stared at each other.

Her heart slammed against her rib cage, she couldn't catch her breath, and her inner voice bombarded her with fragmented thoughts and fears.

Please don't ask if you don't want to hear the answer.

Please don't ask if you don't want to hear the answer.

Please don't—of course he doesn't want to hear the real answer. Light years out of your league. Remember?

Idiot. I'm an idiot.

The voices stopped the moment he reached for her. He brushed his fingers across her cheekbone before slipping them into her hair.

She trembled, part of her wondering if this was what prey felt like the moment before the predator struck.

"What will you miss the most? The forest? The freedom?" He leaned in slightly, his mouth quirking into a smile that made her insides quiver. "Don't tell me it's the bark spiders."

She laughed softly. "Ugh. No. Definitely not them. It's not a what I'll miss. It's who."

"Do I get to know the name of this person?" he teased. She could tell by the heat in his eyes he already knew the answer. Holy hell. He knew, and he wasn't pulling away. She should move right now. Step back and lay out all the reasons this couldn't happen. Only she didn't.

Screw it. She'd already gone this far. Why not go all the way? She laid her hand lightly on his chest and whispered a single word. "You."

"*Re'veth,*" he swore softly, his eyes still locked on hers. "I was afraid you'd say that." Then his fingers tightened in her hair and tugged her head back. His other arm caught her around the waist and pulled her up hard against him.

Then he growled her name just before his mouth crashed down on hers, and the world around them vanished in a blast of white-hot heat.

She moaned, closed her eyes, and kissed him back.

8

———

Until this moment, Axe believed nothing could break him. He'd survived wars, endured abuse at the hands of his corporate owners, and withstood years of solitude and experiments on Reamus Research Station.

He was wrong.

The moment Rin confessed that she would miss him, he broke. He hauled her into his arms and gave in to the desires that had built up over the last few days. He savored the taste of her lips and the lush softness of her curves where they fit against him. Her hair felt like spun silk against his roughened hands, and her mouth was sweeter than honey.

Her moan of desire fanned the flames of his need for her. She'd been a constant presence in his mind since they'd met. She was a collection of intriguing contradictions—a scientific mind combined with a caring heart and a cheerful outlook on life. He'd never known anyone like her. It was easy to relax around her, to joke and laugh in ways he'd observed but never experienced for himself.

Now he'd had a taste, he wanted more. When it came to Rin, he wanted *everything*.

Needs he'd forced himself to deny for years roared to life like rocket fuel poured over the embers of a dying fire.

Her small hand moved to the collar of his shirt, catching hold of it and twisting it around her fingers as she rose up on her toes to kiss him back. He guided her to the nearest tree and pressed her up against it. His mouth never left hers as he shifted his grip on her waist and hair, drawing his hands down over her breasts and the leather straps that held the pauldron in place on her shoulder. One by one, he unbuckled the straps, freeing her breasts from beneath the leather. He palmed them through her shirt, feeling the warm weight in his hands. Her nipples tightened to hard peaks beneath his touch.

Rin arched her back and uttered a low, breathy moan that threatened to shatter what was left of his wits. Then she reached between them to cup the bulge of his cock in her hand, and he was lost.

"Rin," he groaned her name as she gripped him through the fabric of his pants. Not even he was sure what he meant by it. Was it a warning or a demand she continue?

"Yes," was all she said.

It was enough.

Or it would have been... if Amun hadn't chosen that moment to bombard him with images accompanied by a sense of urgent uncertainty Axe translated as *"What is this and what should I do about it?"*

"This better be important, bird!" he spoke the words aloud, so Rin knew about the interruption.

"One image at a time, Hera. I can't focus when you send them that fast," Rin said at almost the same moment.

Apparently, both their companions were determined to ruin the moment. "This is why I was happy on my own," he muttered, his mood darkening quickly. "No one around to interrupt me."

Rin laughed and pulled him in for one last kiss. "If you were by yourself right now, there'd be nothing to interrupt."

And just like that, his anger vanished.

They both lapsed into silence as they tried to make out what their companions were trying to convey. It took him a few seconds, but only because he'd never seen a drone from this angle before. The phrase, a bird's-eye-view, suddenly took on new meaning.

"Son of starbeast. That's an IAF reconnaissance drone," he said out loud while layering on more information for Amun.

"Is that what they are? Douglas is really pushing his luck. Isn't he? Oh, and Hera says there are two of them."

A wicked thought occurred to Axe, and he broke into a grin. "Think our feathered friends would like to play with the lieutenant's new toys?"

Rin's eyes widened, and she clapped her hands with unrepentant glee. "Why don't we ask them?"

Amun, Hera, and the rest of the subjects were more than happy to go after anything the IAF owned, and Rin had to talk fast to convince Hera to wait until the two of them were in the open so they could watch.

Rin grabbed her viewing glasses out of her pack and scanned the sky. "Where are they?"

"Target one is at your four o'clock. Target two is at eight o'clock. It looks like Amun and Hera are going after the second one."

"Thank you. I see them now. You've got amazing vision."

"Cyborg, remember?" He tapped his chest with his fist. "I'm stuffed full of the best technology available eight years ago."

"Eight years?" Rin spun around to stare at him in shock, the pending battle above forgotten.

"What?" He hadn't a clue why she was looking at him like that.

"You're eight years old. Holy hells and gravity wells, that makes me the queen of the cradle robbers!"

He snorted. Of all the things to worry about, that was her concern? "Physically, I'm in my early thirties. I came out of my maturation tank as a fully functional soldier, with all the skills and knowledge I needed. My technical age is irrelevant."

She didn't look convinced, so he added, "Besides, the Vardarians live for centuries and some of them have found cyborg mates. None of that matters here."

He enjoyed watching her expression as she processed what he'd said and realized he was right.

Before she could say anything more, several hawks screamed in challenge and went on the attack. One by one, the hawks dove at the drones, each strike threatening to knock the machines out of the air.

Chunks of debris and shattered housing fell to the

ground after each successful hit, and the entire skirmish ended quickly. The last drone fell in a drunken spiral that ended when it crashed into a tree.

Amun sent a pulse of smug satisfaction that made Axe chuckle. "You wrecked them, bird. Good job," he said out loud.

Rin smiled too, but her eyes moved from the downed drones to the hawks and back several times. "They took them apart so fast." She tapped her chin thoughtfully and looked skyward again before continuing. "You said you were born with the skills and knowledge you needed to fulfill your function. Do you think the same thing could have been done to them? I've worked with predatory birds from various planets and ecologies for years, and I've never seen anything like that. In your opinion as a combat veteran, were they using combat tactics against these things?"

Axe pulled up the recording he'd automatically made and replayed it with her question in mind. Once he stripped away his enjoyment of the spectacle and focused on the fight, the answer to her question was as clear as the sky above.

"Yes, they were." There wasn't a doubt in his mind. Amun and the others had assessed the target, made a plan, and followed through. They'd been created to be weapons... just like him.

"Dammit. That's what I thought, too, but I haven't had hard proof until now, so I've been able to keep that information out of all my reports because it was just a theory. Now..."

She didn't need to finish. He understood. Douglas

had deployed those drones to spy on them. Now there was a good chance the lieutenant had seen more than he bargained for—footage that suggested the birds were exactly what the IAF wanted.

They called down Amun and Hera while the other two birds stayed aloft, looking for more "toys" to play with.

All thoughts of what they'd started in the forest fell to the wayside for the moment. They'd have to revisit that kiss again but not until they'd dealt with this new problem.

If the hawks were what he suspected, the IAF would never let them go, and the rest of the galaxy would consider them too dangerous to live. If Amun and the others had any chance at gaining their freedom, he and Rin would need proof, a plan, and the support of Haven's leadership council. And they needed to come up with it *fast*.

9

———

RIN's thoughts raced around her head like grains of rice tossed into a tornado. Everything she'd suspected about the hawks was true. Axe had kissed her. She needed to keep Hera and the others safe somehow. Holy *fraxx*, that had been some kiss. Had anyone seen the drone footage yet? Had she really been ready to climb the sexy cyborg like a tree and to hell with the consequences? Did she trust Axe enough to tell him everything?

She latched on to that last thought. She trusted Axe completely. Not just because of her attraction to him, or his bond to Amun, but because she knew he was a good, honorable man. He'd help her protect the psy-hawks. And maybe, when this was over, she'd get to kiss him again.

Stars, she hoped so.

It took most of the morning to share everything she suspected but had been keeping a secret. Some of it he already knew, thanks to his connection to Amun, but he didn't know how much information Rin had hidden from the IAF.

She explained everything: the hawks' abilities, their level of intelligence, and their deep aversion to anyone with what she thought of as a military mindset. Combined with what they'd witnessed today, she was certain they'd been intended as military assets, biological versions of drones like the ones they'd destroyed today.

"You're saying that Amun bonded to me because I used to be a scout? We have compatible skill sets?" Axe didn't look happy about that idea.

"I don't think so. Hera bonded to me, after all. I've got next to nothing in common with you when it comes to skills and experience. Not to mention the hawks have had negative reactions to every soldier they've met."

"True." He reached out to stroke Amun's back. "Do you think it's possible their programming was as jacked up as ours? The cyborgs, I mean. This was a private project, right? So the asshole who did this probably didn't have the time or resources for a full-scale experiment. If the first ones to hatch were a failure by their standards, they might have just left the others in cryo-storage until they had time to rework the whole project. Whoever did this never made another attempt."

It was an intriguing theory and meshed with her own suspicions. "I think that's the most likely explanation. The problem is that now the IAF knows about them. If they figure out what they're capable of, there will be a lot of pressure to try to alter their behavioral programming to accept whatever companion the military wants them to have."

Axe slashed at the air with one hand. "That isn't going to happen. These are intelligent beings who deserve to live free and unmolested. I won't allow anyone to do to them what was done to me and my brethren."

"Agreed. But how do we protect them? We need a plan. I've got a few ideas I've been considering, but there are still gaps. They'll need a permanent home where the IAF can't reach them. Whoever takes that on will have to be willing to protect them. Not all the hawks are here, either. A male and female are still at the base where they were discovered."

"They're protecting a potential asset by holding some in reserve."

"Exactly. And getting those two back won't be easy."

Axe waggled one hand from side to side, his lips parting in a sly grin. "That depends. They won't give up a possible weapon without a fight, but if they think this project is a failure..."

"That might work," she agreed.

"It *will* work. We just need to hammer out the details." He looked at her intently, his next words spoken in deep, measured tones. "Victorious warriors win first and then go to war while defeated warriors go to war first and then seek to win."

She cocked her head to one side. "That's a long-winded way of saying he who plans wins."

"You summed it out nicely. The original quote is from an ancient human work called the *Art of War*."

"Ah. I guess that's something your creators included as part of your programmed skills and knowledge?"

He chuckled and shook his head. "No. I just like to read."

Reading wasn't something she imagined him doing much of. Axe seemed more like the active sort, always busy in his workshop or out patrolling the lands around the colony. It reminded her that there was still so much about this man she didn't know. For now, it was enough that she trusted him. There wasn't enough time for anything else.

"I still think I should go with you." Axe stood with his arms folded across his broad chest. Amun was perched on his shoulder, and both of them were glaring at her. They were close to the border where her escort waited but far enough away to talk privately.

"That would only complicate things. It's better if we stick to the routine and act as if nothing out of the ordinary happened." She made a show of holding up both hands and crossing her fingers. "If we get really lucky, no one was monitoring the drones."

Axe shook his head. "Your optimism is adorable."

To her surprise, he caught her by the hands and tugged her toward him as Amun chittered in annoyance and took flight. "If luck were with us today, those damned drones would have shown up *after* we finished our moment in the woods."

He leaned down and kissed her before she could say anything. This time, his lips brushed hers tenderly, lingering just long enough to make her want more. Then he moved away, leaving her breathless and just a little dizzy.

"What was that for?" she asked.

"Because I wanted to know if your lips were as sweet as I remember."

"Oh." She had no idea what to say next. Her mind was a total blank. Though she was certain they'd been arguing about something.

"Shall we go meet your escort?" he asked so smoothly she almost agreed before her brain rebooted and remembered what they'd been discussing—all the reasons why he shouldn't come with her.

"Nice try. You only managed to melt a few of my brain cells. I still remember why you need to stay here."

He winked at her. "It was worth a shot. My friends swear that's the only way they win any arguments with their human mates."

"Your friends lied to you. Us human women are much too smart for that to work."

"We'll see. That was just my first attempt."

"And you are welcome to keep trying. In fact, I encourage it." She tipped her head toward the boundary. "But for now, I have to go. I'll be back after lunch. If I'm not back at the usual time, you have my permission to storm into camp and find me."

The look he gave her was commanding, confident, and undeniably sexy. "If you aren't back on time, I won't need your permission, sunshine. I'll come for you no matter where you are."

"I'm good with that." She waved and set off toward her waiting escort.

Despite her act, Rin expected trouble when she arrived. Douglas was always unhappy about something. Today's list would just be longer.

Lunch turned out to be sandwiches with a double helping of ego on the side. She ate her meal in silence as Douglas seethed and raged about the lost drones. The surprising thing was, he blamed Axe.

"That *fraxxing* cyborg is going to answer for this. The land may belong to him—though so far I can't get anyone on the council to confirm that's the case—but even if he owns the land, he doesn't own the sky."

Rin ate in silence, waiting for Douglas to finish. She still wasn't sure why he thought Axe was responsible. Had none of the hawks appeared in the footage? She hardly dared to hope that was the case.

Douglas slapped the table near her plate. "Dr. Rey, I want an explanation!"

The transition from rant to inquiry was so sudden it took her a few seconds to form a good response. She'd only get one shot at setting this up.

"I'd like an explanation too, Lieutenant. Are you telling me that you ordered those drones to spy on me? First I discover you're tracking me and now this?"

Douglas's expression turned into a confused combination of surprise, outrage, and what she thought might be guilt.

Gotcha, asshole.

"It was a security precaution. You're taking too many risks with the subjects and your own safety."

"I would never endanger the subjects. That would be unprofessional and unforgiveable." *Like using military hardware to spy on people without their permission,* she thought.

"That is not your decision to make. It's mine."

"Yet you never mentioned this to me. Nor did you tell me I'd be under surveillance. When the subjects noticed the drones, they let us know about them. Axe and I assumed the drones belonged to an unknown third party and removed them. I intended to report them to you once I returned to camp. Now you're telling me they were IAF property, but how was I supposed to know that? I did what I thought was necessary to protect the subjects and the project."

The best part about that statement was that most of it was more or less true.

"You thought..." Douglas trailed off, his face reddening.

Rin went back to eating. "When I see Axe this afternoon, I'll let him know who the drones belonged to."

"Send him a message instead."

She swallowed the last bite of her meal before asking. "Why? I'm going back out this afternoon. The other pair of subjects need their exercise."

"You and the subjects are confined to camp for the rest of the day. A dangerous storm is coming this way. High winds, thunder, lightning, hail, and heavy rainfall. It's not safe."

She'd seen the reports already and knew the storm

wasn't due to arrive until tonight. This was pure pettiness on Douglas's part. "The storm is still hours away."

"The weather on this planet can be unpredictable. You are to stay in camp, Dr. Rey. That is my final decision."

She got to her feet. "I think you're forgetting something. This project is on a tight schedule. I have procedures that must be done this afternoon with the second pair of subjects. Because you insisted that one pair stay in camp at all times, I've been unable to observe all the subjects at once."

"You're telling me that you can't miss a single day? Nonsense."

"No. I'm telling you that partial data isn't enough when working with only a few subjects, and we're running out of time."

Douglas flicked his hand in a dismissive gesture. "If you leave against my advice, you'll be on your own. I won't order my men to take unnecessary risks."

She couldn't believe her luck. No security detail meant the birds would be more comfortable, and she could start observing them the moment they left camp.

"I'm here to do a job, and I will perform it to the best of my abilities. That means I have to go back out this afternoon."

"Then go. I'd task a drone to keep watch, but your pet cyborg destroyed the only ones we had."

She didn't rise to the bait. Instead, she gathered up the remains of her meal and tossed it all into the recycling unit. She still had time left on her break but saw no reason not to go back early. She just needed a few minutes to check on her subjects and release the two due for some exercise. Oh, and to remove the tracking devices she'd found in several pieces of her field equipment. She'd had enough of Douglas spying on her.

The sooner she got out of this camp and away from the controlling, arrogant asshole, the happier she'd be.

10

———

Axe returned home after Rin went back to camp. Once there, he went straight to his shop. The hours he spent with her each day had put him behind on several projects, and he usually spent this time doing some work.

He'd been up late every night, too. His medi-bots allowed him to go for days without sleep, and thoughts of Rin had danced through his mind every time he closed his eyes. Staying busy was better than thinking about things he was sure he'd never have, so he'd work until Amun complained about the light and noise.

The hawk had taken over his workshop and now considered it his domain with Axe more of a tolerated guest. At least, that's how Amun saw things. Axe's version of reality was quite different, but most of the time, he let the bird have his delusions.

All attempts to get any work done failed as his thoughts returned time and again to that kiss in the woods. If those drones hadn't shown up... *Veth*, he got hard just thinking about what could have happened. Like all male cyborgs, his corporate creators had ramped up his hormones to make him more aggressive. They hadn't considered what that would do to someone like him, whose purpose was to operate alone.

By the time the war ended, he'd learned to ignore his physical needs. He'd controlled them for years by this point in his life... until Rin. Now she was all he could think about, even when he needed to focus on the higher priority mission—protecting the psy-hawks from the military, and anyone else who wanted to possess and control them.

Axe eventually gave up on working and went inside to eat. Amun followed him and settled on top of the open door. That worked for now when the weather was warm, but Axe made a note to build a proper perch for the hawk before winter.

He retrieved a plate full of roasted *tumpa* out of the cooler and carved off a few slices for himself as well as one for Amun.

"You caught it, so it's only fair you get to enjoy it, too." He tossed the slice to the hawk, who caught it in his beak and proceeded to tear into it. The bird had quickly learned to enjoy cooked meat, a fact Axe had no intention of sharing with Rin. She'd probably lecture him about Amun's dietary requirements. When it came to the hawks, she was as protective as any mother in the wild. It was one of the many things he liked about her. Her kind heart and cheerful disposition were almost as tempting as her kisses. Almost.

He shook his head to free himself from thoughts about the pretty scientist and back to the crisis at hand.

They needed allies, something Rin wouldn't find among the military. That meant any help would have to come from Haven.

It was time he made some calls.

He considered contacting Striker, a friend and the leader of the rangers, but decided to go straight to one of the few cyborgs with real power in the colony. He didn't know Edge well, but he respected him and trusted he would understand what was at stake. He'd been the leader of the cyborgs while they were prisoners and was one of the cyborgs chosen to sit on the leadership council.

He could have reached out via the internal comm channels all cyborgs on Haven shared. He didn't. He opted to send a text message summarizing the situation and ended it with a request to contact him when Edge was free.

He might respect the man, but he was also aware Edge had a temper and his own way of doing things. This way might take longer, but it was more likely to bring Edge on board. If not, he'd have to go to River for help... and that would piss off Edge for sure. Axe had no idea what the deal was between those two, but when they were together, sparks flew. What kind of sparks exactly was anyone's guess.

That done and lunch made, he carried his plate over to the table to eat.

He never got to finish his meal.

One second he had a mouthful of food and a head full of ideas about how to protect the hawks, and the next he was charging out the door with Amun screaming in his head and out loud.

Rin was in danger.

The beast came out of nowhere.

One second Rin was walking through the woods and the next she was fighting for her life… and losing.

Hera and the other hawks did their best to fend off the predator. They attacked it continuously, tearing at its face and slashing at its body while buffeting it with their wings. Rin did the best she could, beating away claws and teeth and yelling until her voice was hoarse.

If she could have run, she might have made it to a tree and climbed it the way Axe had told her to do. None of the local predators could climb well, but right now, neither could she. The initial attack had left her crippled, her left leg shredded from hip to knee by the animal's claws.

The pain was there, but it was a distant thing, easily ignored while she fought to stay alive. When she raised her hands to fend off the cat-like creature, they were coated in blood. She didn't know if belonged to her or her attacker, but there was so much of it she knew one of them was in a lot of trouble.

This is how I die. The thought came to her with crystalline clarity, despite the chaos of the moment. Even knowing it was probably true, Rin didn't stop fighting. She needed to stay alive. There was so much more she needed to learn about the psy-hawks and about Axe. She wasn't ready to die. She wanted to live. To find out if that kiss could lead to something more.

The next time she tried to raise her arms to ward off an attack, only one of them moved. She saw the gap in her defenses at the same time the predator did, and for a moment they stared at each other.

This was the end. She knew it. All she could do was look death in the face and scream in defiance, so that's what she did.

Only another sound drowned her out. A primal roar of challenge tore through the air, and Hera sent her a single image accompanied by a powerful surge of hope. The image was of Axe, the blade of his axe raised high over his head as he charged headlong through the trees.

The hawks fought until the last minute and then rose into the air as something huge and snarling slammed into the creature. Axe. He struck with enough force to knock it away from her, and she got a brief glimpse of him as he crossed through her rapidly narrowing field of vision.

Darkness crowded the edges of her vision as she collapsed onto the ground, the last of her strength draining away. She stared up at the canopy of trees above her, unable to move. The forest was beautiful from this angle, and Hera was in her head, sending thoughts of encouragement and concern.

Rin sent back thoughts of consolation and gratitude. Then the pain finally hit her in an agonizing flood that drowned out every thought but one. She had to see Axe one more time. If this was the end, she wanted to go looking at the face of the man she could have fallen in love with... if only they'd had more time.

Hera landed beside her, one taloned foot resting

lightly on her shoulder as the bird chirped softly in distress.

"Axe okay?" she whispered.

Hera responded with a bob of her head Rin had learned was their version of a nod. If Axe was alive, the beast was dead. Good.

"If I die, you should stay with Amun and Axe." Rin wasn't sure if she actually spoke the words aloud or just held them in her mind. Either way, she hoped Hera understood. This place was safe, and Axe would take care of Hera.

The scientific part of Rin's brain wanted to consider the ramifications of a bonded pair losing one of the partners and was frustrated she wouldn't be around to find out. The rest of her just fought to stay awake long enough to see Axe.

She heard him hurry toward her, his footfalls hard and heavy.

"Rin!" She opened her eyes when he spoke her name and saw him leaning over her, his beard and face smeared with blood and his eyes dark with worry.

"You were right," she whispered softly. "I should have let you come with me."

"Yes, you should have." He moved over her as he talked, every touch of his hands sending fresh waves of pain surging through her body. "That won't happen again. I'm not leaving your side, sunshine. You hear me? You're not to go *anywhere* without me."

She reached up to touch his blood-splattered face but couldn't lift her arm high enough. He saw what she wanted, though, and caught her hand in his much larger one, raising it to his cheek.

"Take care of Hera. Please?" Her words were soft and sounded mushy even to her own ears. Darkness filled her vision until he was the only thing she could see.

"You're not listening to me. You aren't going anywhere without me. That includes the *fraxxing* afterlife." Axe squeezed her fingers and glared down at her. "Stay with me, Rin."

"Want to. Don't think. I can."

"Yes, you can. There's a way. You can stay here, but I need your permission."

She didn't understand what he meant, but she managed the faintest of nods and whispered, "I want... to stay. Please. Help me. Stay."

"I will, sunshine. All you have to do is hang on." He bent down to kiss her forehead. "I'm sorry, Rin. This next part is going to hurt."

Before she could ask what was next, something wrapped around her injured leg and squeezed. As the pressure increased, so did the pain. She fought to free herself from the source of the agony, but she couldn't make it stop. She heard a scream of pain that might have been her own. Then the darkness enveloped her.

11

____

AXE HAD SEEN ENOUGH of war and its aftermath to recognize a potentially mortal wound when he saw one. Rin's left leg had been torn up so badly he could see glimpses of white bone beneath the river of scarlet blood flowing from the slashed flesh.

If he could get her to a med-center, they'd be able to do something, but would it be enough? Rin was an ordinary human with no nanotech or cybernetics to help her recover.

Fraxx, she couldn't even block pain the way he could. She had to be suffering, but all she'd asked for was him to take care of Hera. Selfless, reckless fool. Why had she been out here alone? Where was her damned security detail when she actually needed one?

He tore through her pack until he found the basic first aid kit he knew she carried. He used the canister of wound sealant on her injuries starting with the areas above the tourniquet. Then he used every bandage in the kit to make a field dressing. It was the best he could do, but it wouldn't be enough.

Fear and frustration tore through him as he cradled Rin's limp body in his arms. She'd passed out when he'd used his belt as a tourniquet for her leg, and the remains of his shirt were now wadded up against the dressing on her hip. He held her so her injured side was pressed against him. It was the only way he could think of to continue applying pressure while he got her to the only place where she could get the help she needed, including some that would come at a high cost for both of them.

She'd have her life but lose her freedom, and she might blame him for it. He looked down at Rin's pale, beautiful face and knew his decision was already made. If saving her meant she never forgave him? So be it.

He broke into a run, sprinting through the trees so quickly the hawks fell behind. "*Going home,*" he sent to Amun. "*Bring the others.*"

It only took a few minutes at his maximum speed to reach his home. Rin stirred and moaned once or twice, but never regained consciousness. Her silence spurred him on as he realized how much he enjoyed listening to her talk about the hawks, the project, and just about anything else she was passionate about. After a lifetime of solitude, he'd found someone he enjoyed spending time with. Now, the universe wanted to take her away from him. The universe could *fraxx* right off. Rin belonged with him. He would not let her go.

He held on to that thought as he opened an internal comm channel he'd never used before—the one that linked him to every cyborg in the colony.

"This is Axe. I need help." With that confession out of the way, he went on to explain the situation: Rin's injury, their current location, his concerns about Lieutenant Douglas, and why he didn't want the officer informed about what had happened until Rin was stable.

He had no idea who would answer his call for help. To many of the cyborgs, he was little more than a name.

The response stunned him. Acknowledgments flooded in from everyone. Every single cyborg on the planet offered to assist. It almost overwhelmed him.

Then a single message came through as a priority. It was Edge.

"I'm coordinating the response. River will bring the human doctor to you. Wreckage and Ruin are closest to you, so I've dispatched them to check the scene of the attack and secure it against contamination by the human soldiers," he informed Axe.

"Thank you. Oh, and tell those two to bring me back my axe. It's still with the body of the ghost cat."

"Done. What else do you need," Edge said.

"A fresh vial of medi-bots. I don't think she'll survive without them."

Edge fell silent so long Axe wondered if his request would be denied. If Edge refused, he'd try injecting Rin with some of his blood. It might work... but his nanotech was coded to his DNA. The newer medi-bots could be given to anyone.

"You know that's not how things work," Edge said. *"Humans need to be vetted before being accepted as citizens, and non-citizens are never offered the nanotech."*

"*You asked me what I need. I need* her. *Do you understand?*"

"*I think so.*" Another pause. "*I'll bring it over myself. There's going to be hell to pay when the military learns what we've done. You ready for that?*"

Despite everything, Axe grinned to himself. "*Are you asking me if I'm ready for a fight? I think we both know the answer to that.*"

Edge chuckled. "*Yeah. We do. Keep her alive until we get there.*"

"*I will.*"

He charged the last stretch to his home and almost kicked the door off its hinges as he barreled inside with Rin still in his arms.

"Help is on the way, sunshine. Oh, and welcome to my home. You're the first person to ever visit."

Until today, he'd never allowed anyone inside, not even the handful of friends who knew where he lived. Now, everyone knew where to find him, and in a few minutes, his quiet home would be filled with the chaos and noise that always came with a crowd.

The thought didn't bother him as much as he expected.

Rin woke to the unfamiliar sounds of people talking in hushed tones somewhere nearby. Who the hell were they and why were they in her habi-pod? When she opened her eyes, she quickly developed a new set of questions. Where the hell was *she*, and why was she here?

"Hello?" her voice was little more than a husky rasp, but it was enough to get someone's attention.

"You're awake!" She recognized Axe's voice right away. But why did he sound so relieved?

"Awake but confused," she said as she struggled to open her eyes.

Then Hera was in her head, sending her a flood of emotions. Happiness, worry, and more relief. Why was everyone so happy she was awake?

Hera sent her several images that explained everything. The first one showed her fighting with a large predator. The next was of her lying on the forest floor, her leg shredded and blood everywhere. The last one was of Axe standing over the corpse of the animal that attacked her, his blood-splattered axe gripped in his hand.

"Thank you, Hera. I remember now," she said aloud and then turned to look at Axe.

"You saved me."

"The hawks saved you. They kept the ghost cat distracted long enough for me to reach you. I just finished the job."

"He also treated your wounds at the scene, carried you back here, and then called for help. I'm Dr. Clark and I was part of the group that came to assist you," someone new joined the conversation and Rin moved her head enough to catch sight of the speaker. A human woman with graying brown hair and a warm smile stood not far from Axe.

"Hi, Doctor." She had to force the next words out past her suddenly tight throat. "Did I lose the leg? I know it was bad..."

Axe smiled tightly. "You're still in one piece, sunshine."

"Yes, you are. I wish I could take credit for that, but all I did was regenerate your lesser injuries and treat you for shock and pain. The rest..." She looked at Axe and gave him an approving smile. "You can thank Axe for that."

Rin looked at Axe, but the big man avoided her gaze. "Axe? What happened?"

The doctor cleared her throat. "I think that's our cue to leave. We'll be downstairs with the others. I'm sure they'll want to hear the good news."

She caught sight of several others as they retreated. None of them looked familiar. Two were Vardarian males, along with at least two more cyborgs—one male and one female. "Thank you," she managed to raise her voice enough to be heard as they left.

Once they were alone, Rin gingerly sat up and looked around. "I see Hera and Amun, but where are the other subjects? Are they okay?" she asked.

"Douglas lost his mind when he found out what happened. He wanted both you and the hawks returned to his camp immediately. The doctor told him that wasn't going to happen, and she was more qualified than a field medic to deal with your injuries. We had to send the hawks back, though. Douglas insisted. They headed out before the storm hit. Hera and Amun confirmed their safe arrival."

Hearing that the other subjects were safe eased some of the knots in her stomach. The rest of the knots would have to wait until Axe explained things.

She raised the blanket to check and determined that she had on one of Axe's shirts and not much else. *Fraxx*, who had undressed her? She hoped it had been the lady doctor, but a small part wondered if it had been Axe... and if he'd liked what he'd seen.

She decided to blame that entirely inappropriate thought on whatever pain blockers she'd been given and tried to focus on more practical matters, like taking stock of her surroundings. Sunlight streamed through a pair of windows, one of which was open to let in a warm breeze. Instead of a wall, the other side of the room had a railing. Hera and Amun were perched on it, both of them watching her intently.

Beyond the rail and the hawks was a vaulted ceiling over what she assumed was a living area of some kind. The wall ahead of her had a large, elegantly carved wardrobe and a door that led into a room with tiled floors. Probably a sanitation room. An open archway was cut into the wall beside the bed, leading into yet another room. A walk-in closet maybe? That didn't seem likely for a man with Axe's practical tastes.

His home wasn't what she'd envisioned at all. She'd expected something more rustic and simple. Once Axe had explained things, she was eager to look around.

That's when it finally struck her. She had no pain. She felt fine. Better than that, even. She felt amazing.

"Remind me to ask the doctor what pharma she gave me. I'm clear headed and pain free. I didn't know that was possible."

Axe cleared his throat and then sat down on the bed beside her. "It's not. I mean, the doctor gave you something for the pain yesterday, but it should be out of your system by now."

"Yesterday?" That couldn't be right. The attack had only been a few hours ago. Hadn't it?

He gently covered her hand with his, and she twisted it so she could twine their fingers together. "Tell me what's going on. Please."

"The attack was yesterday afternoon. You passed out when I put the tourniquet on your leg and didn't come fully awake again until now. It's midmorning."

"I've been out for most of a day?"

"You have. Hera has stayed with you since I brought you here. Amun's hunted for both of them, but she's refused to eat."

Rin glanced over at her hawk. "You need to eat, Hera. Go. I'm okay."

The hawk bobbed her head, launched herself off the rail, and flew out the open window. Amun followed her.

"Those two are closer than ever," she observed. "That might be a problem when I go."

Axe's fingers tightened around hers. "About that. You, uh." He paused to scrub a hand through his beard, swore softly, and continued. "You can't leave."

"What? Why not? Wait, you mean I can't go right away because I'll need time to recover?"

"No." He turned to look at her with haunted eyes and a grim expression. "Do you remember anything after the attack? We had a conversation before you lost consciousness."

Rin racked her brain, trying to remember. She'd

wanted to see his face again before she died. "I remember bits of it."

"Good. I asked you to stay with me. You said you wanted to. I may have taken that as permission."

"To do what?" she asked.

"To save your life the only way I knew how. We had to dose you with medi-bots. You're not in pain because you are almost fully healed already." He waited a beat before explaining further.

"The doctor consulted with some Vardarian healers to confirm everything was in order. You're only a few hours away from a full recovery."

Rin opened and closed her mouth several times as she tried to process what he'd told her. "I have nanotech?"

"You do. I'm sorry I did that without your permission. I..." He trailed off, but she got the sense he wanted to say more.

"You saved me! Don't you dare apologize for that." She grabbed a handful of his shirt and pulled him in close. "I'm alive because of what you did. Thank you."

Then she kissed him. She'd meant it to be a light kiss of gratitude, but the moment their lips touched, it became something more. Heat flooded her veins as Axe growled her name softly and kissed her back.

It all felt too perfect, like a dream she'd wake up from any second. She was safe, whole, and in bed with Axe.

"Yes," she whispered against his lips.

He tore his mouth from hers with a frustrated sigh. "Actually, no. Not yet." He pointed toward the floor. "I have a house full of beings at the moment, and most of them have cybernetically enhanced hearing."

As if on cue, chuckles erupted from below.

"Cyborg hearing sucks," she muttered.

"It's not fun for us, either!" someone called back.

"That's Wreckage. He's an asshole." Axe raised his voice. "And it's about time everyone went home. Thanks for your help. Talk to you all later. Bye now."

Rin buried her face in the crook of Axe's neck, too embarrassed to say anything else.

"Rin says thanks, too," Axe added. "Oh, and can someone let that trumped up twit of a lieutenant know Dr. Rey is awake and expected to make a full recovery?"

"Already done," the doctor called out with only a hint of laughter in her voice. "I take it we're not sharing the details of her condition yet?"

"We are not," Axe confirmed.

"Hell no," someone else chimed in. "The leadership council needs to meet and come up with a plan before we tell the IAF we're keeping their scientist."

"That's Edge," Axe told her softly. "He's on the council, and he's the one who okayed your medi-bot treatment."

"Remind me to thank him later." She raised her head to give him a small smile. "Much later." She still had a lot to process. Her near-death experience, her new enhanced status, and the fact that the nanotech might mean she couldn't leave the planet for the foreseeable future. It would take time to come to terms with it all, but for now, she just wanted to celebrate being alive.

And she wanted to do it with the man who'd saved her twice in one day.

12

———

He'd expected confusion and anger once he told her what he'd done. After all he'd been through, he knew the value of consent and the pain that came when your choices were taken away. And that's exactly what he'd done to Rin. She had every right to be furious with him, but instead she was nestled in his arms, kissing him with a passion that made it hard to think of anything but how much he wanted her.

Was this why some of the others complained they didn't understand their women? He suspected it was, but right now, he didn't care. All that mattered was that Rin wasn't angry with him. In fact, she was anything but unhappy right now, and he intended to keep it that way.

"You're supposed to take it easy for the rest of the day. Doctor's orders." He kissed her softly and then moved back enough to be able to look her in the eyes. "So, if we're doing this, you need to promise me you'll tell me if anything hurts or you need to stop. I don't want to hurt you, sunshine."

"You'd never hurt me."

Re'veth. She meant that. This sweet, incredible woman wasn't afraid of him at all. "I'd never hurt you intentionally. But you're tiny and delicate."

She laughed. "Only you would see me that way. And I'm not delicate! Thanks to you, I have medi-bots. I'm almost immortal!"

Her smile faltered. "Holy *fraxx*. That's exactly what I am. Isn't it? I'm going to live for centuries."

He braced himself for the anger he'd expected earlier. "You will. I... I know that must be a shock."

She beamed. "It's amazing! Don't you see? I have decades of research to do on the hawks. It's a lifetime's worth of work and now I have several lifetimes to do it."

"That's one way to think about it." Once again, he marveled at the way Rin approached things.

"It's the only way to think about it." She raised her hands and then flicked out her fingers as if casting something away. "Oh sure, I could dwell on the fact I'll outlive my friends and family, but that could happen anyway. I could be unhappy about being confined to this planet because that's what the other human colonists agreed to when they came here, and it will probably apply to me, too. But this place is amazing, with new species of birds to be documented, and I'm the only ornithologist on the whole *planet*."

He caught her under the chin with one finger and lifted her head so she was looking at him. "And if you like... you can live here. With me. I've got plenty of space, and Amun seems to like it well enough."

She didn't say anything for several painfully long seconds. *Fraxx.* He shouldn't have said anything.

"Did you just ask me to move in with you? Live with you? In the house no one has ever even visited until today?"

"Yes, I did. And I'm still waiting for your answer."

She gave a soft squeal of delight and hugged him. "Yes. I know it's too soon and we're both crazy, but the answer is yes."

At that moment, he swore he heard the walls around his heart crack. "I don't think I'm crazy. I think I'm falling in love. Though I've heard it's hard to tell the difference."

Rin squeaked. At least, that's the only way he could describe the adorable little sound she made as she peppered his face with kisses.

"I'm falling for you, too. I told myself I couldn't because you were part of my project and because you were so far out of my league you might as well be in a different galaxy."

That stunned him. "Why would you think that? You're lovely, sexy, sweet, and smart as hell."

"Keep saying things like that and you're going to be stuck with me forever."

"Challenge accepted." Axe gathered her close and rose from the bed, lifting her with him.

"Where are we going?"

"It's time we started your tour of our house, my effervescent little beauty." He would need to make a list of compliments for her and use them all. "First stop, the bath."

"That sounds wonderful. I'd love a chance to clean up."

"I thought you might. I'll get the bath running and then give you a few minutes of privacy. Then you and I are going to enjoy a long, hot bath together."

Rin groaned in delight, the sound traveling straight through him and sending all the blood in his body straight to his cock.

"That might be the sexiest thing anyone has ever said to me," she said.

The thought of anyone else saying seductive things to Rin made him growl and grumble under his breath. If anyone even looked at her the wrong way, he'd tear their arm off and beat them with it.

"Whoa. What was that?" she asked.

He shrugged. "I just discovered I'm the jealous type. You're mine, sunshine. No one else gets to talk to you the way I do."

She laughed and patted his cheek. "The same goes for you, growly."

He set her down and kissed the top of her head. If anyone else had called him that, he'd make them regret it. But when Rin said it, he didn't mind at all. That confirmed what he already suspected... he really was in love.

How the *fraxx* had that happened?

The sanitation room was another surprise to Rin. The tiled floors were textured and colored to look like pale beach sand with smooth tiles the same color on the walls. One entire end of the space was an open shower, and next to it was a large, square bath, more than big enough for two. The wall above the tub had a window that let in air and light while providing a view of the forest outside. For a man as rough around the edges as Axe, he certainly liked his personal comforts.

Hot water poured into the tub, blending with a citrusy scented product Axe had added before he left her alone for a few minutes.

The last thing she did before calling Axe back was to pop a quick dissolving dental-tab into her mouth. The mint-flavored foam worked quickly, freshening her breath and cleaning her teeth.

She kept her borrowed shirt on, even though she knew they wouldn't stay dressed for long. Then she picked up several thick, fluffy towels and carried them closer to the bath. With everything ready, she peeked her head into the bedroom to call him... and got her first look through the archway beside the bed.

It was a library. Shelves full of real, physical books lined the walls. She hadn't seen so many in one place since leaving university. Her solitary cyborg was full of surprises.

"The bath is ready," she called.

Axe stepped into view immediately, and he was quite the vision. He was naked, and she allowed herself a few seconds to appreciate the view. The man was impossibly perfect with washboard abs, a trim waist, broad shoulders, and thighs as thick as tree trunks. His chest hair narrowed to a treasure trail that led her eyes down to... *wow*. He was big and thick *all* over.

"You're still dressed," he complained as he moved to join her.

"I uh, thought..." she waved her hands in front of her as she lost the ability to speak.

"No thinking. Not right now." He caught the shirt by the hem and drew it up slowly.

All she had to do was raise her arms and then she was naked. He was right. Now wasn't the time to think. Now was the time to *feel*, and holy hell, she felt so much. She wanted him. Ached for him. Not just his touch or his kisses, but all of him.

She stepped into his arms and pressed her body to his, skin to skin for the first time.

His cock throbbed against her belly as he bent down to kiss her hard. The heat of his mouth and the strength of the arms that closed around her made her dizzy with need, and she kissed him back with all the passion in her soul.

She surrendered control to him and allowed him to guide her to the tub while never breaking their kiss. Then her feet were off the ground as he lifted her into the air and lowered her gently into the water before joining her.

The water was perfect, hot enough to soothe without scalding her skin. They somehow managed to lower themselves into the tub without letting go of each other. Axe leaned against the side of the tub with his legs outstretched while Rin sat facing him with her legs straddling his thighs and her hands on his shoulders for balance.

They looked at each other for a moment in silence, lips only a whisper away from each other's mouth. The air almost crackled with anticipation. This was what she'd wanted since the first time they'd met, and a little voice inside her head told her she'd never stop wanting this... never stop needing him.

"Yes," she whispered, not even sure what she was agreeing to.

"Yes," he answered, and then his mouth was on hers, branding her with his kisses and claiming her body with every touch of his hands.

He palmed her breasts in his hands and raised one leg to press it against her pussy. She moaned into his mouth, arching her back and rocking her hips so she could grind herself against his thigh.

She slid one hand between their slick bodies and wrapped her fingers around the thick length of his hard cock. Axe responded with a shuddering groan that sent her libido into overdrive. Her movements sent water splashing against the sides of the bath, the rolling motion creating currents that threatened her balance.

Axe dropped his hands to her hips to hold her steady, changing the angle of their bodies so that his cock slid across the seam of her pussy.

She used her fingers to part her lower lips, exposing her clit. The first contact made her gasp and shiver as she guided him into the perfect position and held him there while they ground against each other, groaning into each other's mouths as they teased themselves with pleasure.

When she was almost to her breaking point, Axe's grip tightened, and he raised her off his lap, holding her there until she wriggled in protest.

His face broke into a smug grin and he winked as he lowered her slowly onto his cock.

"You're mine, now, sunshine."

A sense of light and wonderment bubbled up inside her, momentarily eclipsing her desires. "Always were. Always will be."

Then passion took over, and she added, "Now fuck me, please."

He drove his hips up as he pulled her toward him, burying himself to the hilt inside her body.

Pleasure bloomed, her entire body shuddering. Her breathing was reduced to ragged gasps and soft pants as he lifted her again and then snapped his hips up in a thrust that put him deep inside again.

"More. Please. Yes." The words fell from her lips as she flexed her body around him, trying to give him as much pleasure as he gave her. They fell into a rhythm, the sounds of sex and need blending with the slosh and slap of the water as they raced each other toward orgasm.

He broke their kiss to bury his face in the side of her neck, nipping and kissing her as he groaned her name.

She clung to him, nails digging into his shoulders, her legs tightening and toes curling as she reached the apex of her climb and tumbled over the edge and into a release that stole her breath and momentarily shattered her mind.

He came soon after, muffling his last cry against her flesh as he emptied himself inside her.

After that, neither of them moved for a long time. She dropped her head to his chest and floated, sated and happier than she could remember. They still had problems to face and questions to answer, but all that could wait a few more hours. For now, she had everything she wanted right here.

13

———

RIN DOZED on his couch while he made them both something to eat. The doctor had mentioned she'd need plenty of protein and calories to regain her strength and help her body finish healing. With that in mind, he made two large omelets with fresh vegetables from the garden and fried up several locally made sausages and slices of the Vardarian version of bacon to go with it.

The food dispenser brewed up a pot of tea and produced several slices of toast slathered with butter. He took one look at the pile and decided to add a more. It was his first time cooking for a guest, and he didn't want to seem stingy.

He brought her a cup of tea and set it down on the table closest to her. He watched her sleep for a few seconds, amazed that this incredible woman was here, in his home and in his life.

"Food is almost ready," he said softly, almost regretting the need to wake her.

Rin yawned and stretched, and his cock went

instantly hard as he envisioned her arching beneath him as he powered into her. He stopped that line of thinking before all his good intentions vanished and he took her right here on the couch.

She had other needs he should see to, like eating and sleeping. She might have medi-bots now, but she was still only human. He'd have to remember that.

"Smells yummy," she said, her voice still muzzy with sleep. Then she perked up. "Is that bacon?"

"It's close enough to make no difference, and it's local," he told her.

"I think I'm really going to like it here. Fresh bacon. Now if you tell me you have fresh eggs, too..."

"I do. I keep a few chickens out back."

She sat up and stared at him. "You have chickens? Here?"

"I have chickens," he confirmed. "Why does this surprise you? I like animals and the colony permits us to have a variety of livestock."

She waved her hands. "It's not that. I haven't seen a chicken since I left my parents' farm. I've missed fresh food so much."

He grinned. "Would now be a good time to mention I have my own garden, too?"

"Be still my heart. You have a library, chickens, and a garden. Anything else I should know?"

"I cooked breakfast myself."

Rin threw a hand to her forehead and pretended to swoon. It was ridiculously dramatic, but he loved it. "That's it. I'm proposing. You are the perfect man."

"Cyborg," he corrected her. "And I'm far from perfect."

Whatever she was about to say was cut off by an intense mental blast that nearly knocked him off his feet.

It was Amun, and whatever was happening, the hawk was frantic about it. So much so that Axe had no idea what the bird was trying to convey.

"*Slower,*" he sent back. "*I cannot comprehend.*"

Rin pinched her nose with her fingers and closed her eyes before saying, "I'm here, Hera. I don't understand what's wrong. Explain slowly."

So whatever it was, both hawks were aware of it, and Axe got the sense it wasn't an immediate threat. At least, not to them. So what was it?

Amun went quiet for several seconds and then sent an image of a hawk. One became two, became three, and soon there were six images. Then two vanished and Amun sent another pulse of alarm. "*Gone! No find.*"

Now he got it. "Two of the hawks are missing. I can't tell which ones. Can Hera tell you?" he asked Rin.

She paused for a few seconds and then nodded. "It's the two you sent back to camp yesterday. Hera says they're gone and she can't find them."

"Amun said the same thing."

Rin jumped to her feet. "What the *fraxx* has that idiot done now? Where are my clothes? We need to go to the camp and find out what the hell is going on."

"Your clothes were ruined. Remember? River brought over a bunch of stuff she thought would fit. I'll get it. You stay here and check your messages. Maybe there's an explanation for this." He didn't believe that for a moment. Rin was right. This had to be Douglas's doing.

He dashed off, but even at his increased speed he didn't make it back to her before Rin howled in fury.

"That asshole! That stupid, arrogant popinjay on a power trip!"

Axe grabbed the entire bundle of clothes and rushed back downstairs. "What happened?"

"Lieutenant *fraxxing* Douglas happened. He knew I was injured and unavailable, but he sent me messages, anyway." Rin's voice was tight with barely controlled rage and her hands shook as he pointed to her comm unit. "According to him, my reckless behavior and disregard for his authority put the entire project at risk. He has therefore decided to end the project early. All personnel, equipment, and test subjects will depart the planet later today. Given my *ongoing resistance to his authority and disregard for security procedures,*" her voice dripped venom at those words, "arrangements will be made for my transport at a later time. That son of a starbeast has basically cut me out of the program and used our argument yesterday to blame me for everything he's doing. The rat bastard."

"And now two of the hawks are missing." Dread sank its claws into his guts and twisted as he considered what Douglas might be up to. None of the answers were good ones.

Rin paled. "What's he done to them?"

"Get dressed and meet me outside. We can figure this out on the way." He left before Rin could say anything else. It would take him a few minutes to get their ride ready, and the clock was ticking.

"What the hell is *that*?" Rin demanded, her voice almost drowned out by the low rumble of the twin engines.

Axe pulled her in for a quick kiss and then handed her a helmet. He waited for her to put it on so they could use the built-in mics to speak instead of yelling. Once she fastened it in place, he pointed at their ride.

"It's a sky-sled. I use it to transport raw logs to my shop and deliver finished products to town. Hop on and strap in. We don't know how much time we have."

She bounded up the ladder and sat down in the jump-seat he'd unfolded along one side of what he considered the cockpit. The vehicle was basically a metal platform welded to a pair of air-bike chassis with the controls for both bikes rerouted to a central dashboard.

"Okay, I'm secured. Let's go!" she said.

Axe had already leaped on board without bothering with the ladder and had them in the air in seconds. Amun and Hera rose with them, both of them screaming battle cries that needed no translation. The hawks were as pissed as their two-legged partners.

They talked through the most likely scenarios on the short flight to the IAF camp. They both agreed that Douglas was using her attack as an excuse to cut the mission short and return to civilization. He'd been unhappy about the assignment since the decision to come to this planet.

What they couldn't work out was what had happened to the two missing subjects. They'd returned to camp safely and should have been secured in their cages. If they'd released themselves to go flying, their link to the others would have faded gradually with the increased distance. They'd just vanished, and the other subjects didn't know where they'd gone.

"I think Douglas saw the drone footage and realized I hadn't told him everything." Rin sighed loudly enough he heard it over their comms. "But that doesn't explain why he's packing up so quickly. All he had to do was send a report back to base. They'd believe him, and it's not like there's some way for anyone to swoop in and take the subjects away from the military. They're too well-guarded."

That's when it hit him. "Guarded from you. Yes. What about from someone on the inside?"

Rin stilled for several seconds and then burst into a string of curses before saying, "That has to be it! He's taken two of them and is going to sell them to the highest bidder. That explains why he's scrambling to leave. He needs to make the deal and disappear before anyone figures out what he's doing. *Fraxxing* bastard. No wonder he didn't want to come to Liberty! It's the only location we considered that doesn't allow ships to enter the atmosphere without proper clearance."

That made sense. Because of the various threats against the colony and its citizens, access to the planet was carefully controlled and monitored. Whoever his buyer was, they were likely blacklisted and wouldn't be able to even approach the planet. "He'll do the exchange outside this system, somewhere no one is watching."

"We can't let him leave." Rin sounded frantic.

"We won't. Like you said, Liberty's air space is carefully controlled. Give me a moment, I'm sending a message to Edge and a few others. They'll arrange for a lockdown of all traffic on and off the planet."

"Ask for backup, too. I can't see the lieutenant letting us ruin his plans without a fight, and his men are all loyal. I wondered why he wanted to pick his own team for this. Now I see. He's planned this since the beginning."

Axe relayed both requests and heard back immediately. Shutting down all traffic wasn't a problem. Getting to the camp in time to help would be an issue. Most of the colony's weapons were stored in bunkers. Apart from the rangers and a few other exceptions, none of the citizens carried firearms of any kind. The Vardarians preferred blades, and the cyborgs were weapons themselves. Going up against armed soldiers with bladed weapons was too risky, and it would take time they didn't have to get everyone armed and organized.

"Get there when you can. I'll try to delay and distract the asshole until you show up."

Edge chuckled. "Sure you will. And when it goes to hell you'll wade in and kill them all before we get a chance to join the fun. Kick ass and stay alive, my friend. We'll see you soon."

My friend. Despite everything, the words made Axe smile. He had more friends than he realized.

They were two minutes out now, close enough that

with his enhanced optics he could see the camp was already partially dismantled. Men hustled here and there, some packing, others loading a military-style shuttle bearing IAF markings.

"*Fraxx.* They've already brought down a shuttle. That will make things trickier." And a lot more dangerous. That was a military shuttle, which meant it would be armed and hardened against weapon fire. It also represented a chance for them all to escape, and there was nothing more dangerous than an armed adversary who thought they had a chance to get away.

"Do you know how to fire a blaster?" he asked.

Rin laughed. "My mom's retired law enforcement. I can shoot just about anything with a trigger."

"Good." He took one hand off the controls and unholstered the plasma pistol he wasn't supposed to have. "Take this. Power bank is full, safety is on. If anyone does something stupid, shoot them."

She took the pistol, gave it a quick once-over, and then nodded in his direction as calm and collected as if she was a seasoned soldier. It was sexy as hell.

"Got it. You think they'll fight?" she asked.

"No idea, but it's better to be prepared for the worst. And you might want to stay out of sight until we know what's going on. They think you're too wounded to move right now. Let's use that to our advantage."

She nodded again, unstrapped herself and hunkered down on the floor, out of sight.

"One more thing, sunshine. Don't get hurt. I don't ever want to go through that again. My heart can't take it."

She flashed him an achingly beautiful smile. "Same goes for you, growly. One day with you is not nearly enough."

The last thing they did was tell the hawks to fly to a safe distance and stay clear. Then, he gunned the engines and dropped the nose so they'd make their final approach hard and fast.

As they descended, it struck him that everything was different this time. He wasn't going into this fight alone. In fact, if things went well, he might never be alone again.

He flew into the camp grinning like a lunatic.

14

Rin knew how to use a weapon like the one Axe had handed her, but she'd never been in a situation where she'd have to use one against another person. That wouldn't stop her from firing if she had to. It was one thing to hope for a peaceful outcome, but Axe was right. It was best to be prepared for things to go sideways.

Hera circled the camp and fed her images. The shuttle wasn't the one they'd flown down in. This one was larger, and she assumed it was the one used for transporting equipment.

She'd almost forgotten about the ship they'd arrived on. It had remained in orbit around the planet with a skeleton crew all this time.

They had to keep Douglas and the others from reaching that ship.

Axe landed the sled in the middle of the camp, the engines sending up clouds of dust and debris. They came to a stop with a thump that made her glad she had a tight grip on the seat she crouched beside.

"Sorry. I got carried away," Axe said. "Stay out of sight for now. Let's see how this plays out."

"Good luck." The need to kiss him was so powerful she almost gave in to it and to hell with the plan, but if Douglas saw her in a lip-lock with Axe, it would probably send him into orbit. Since the goal was to keep him calm and talking until backup got here, she stayed where she was.

Axe's hand strayed to the *kes'tarv* that hung from his belt as if to check it was still there. Then he bent his knees slightly and launched himself into the air. He cleared the side of the sled with ease and vanished from sight, but Hera could still see him. The hawk fed Rin a real-time view that flowed like video. Axe landed some distance from the sled, the dust swirling around his feet and legs. He kept his eyes locked on the shuttle, but she couldn't tell why.

This kind of information from Hera was new. Until now, the hawk had only sent single images. Rin had no idea the hawk could manage this kind of surveillance. It was more evidence that whoever had created these animals had intended for them to be used as spies. They probably never imagined a scenario where their creations would act against the ones trying to control them.

Surprise, assholes.

"Do not take another step, cyborg. You're trespassing on Interstellar Armed Forces land." The voice was immediately recognizable as Douglas's, and Hera shifted her view to pick out the lieutenant standing near the lowered ramp of the shuttle.

He had a hand on his blaster but hadn't removed it from its holster, and his posture was so puffed up he looked like he might explode at any second.

Axe opened his hands in a friendly gesture and took a step forward. "I'm here to relay messages from Dr. Rey. She is awake and has read your messages. She had some concerns about the transportation of the subjects."

"Damn right I do. Starting with where you transported my missing subjects," she muttered under her breath.

"Dr. Rey is no longer attached to this project. She gave up the right to have *concerns* when she disregarded my orders yesterday. Her actions put the subjects at risk."

"Be that as it may, she is still the expert when it comes to these birds. She asked me to see to it that they're all loaded safely onto the shuttle. Once that's done, I'll go. It would set her mind at ease if you would allow me to do that."

Axe sounded calm and reasonable, but she knew it was an act. He'd been angry before they left his house and had only gotten more so on their way here. Douglas blaming her for what happened would only piss him off further.

"I don't give a *fraxx* about the doctor's peace of mind. You're not getting anywhere near the subjects. You've already stolen one. I should have you charged for that."

Axe took another step. Several soldiers appeared from the partially dismantled buildings and took up ready positions to watch the confrontation. They were all armed, but none of them pointed their weapons at Axe...

yet. She hoped it stayed that way. As tough as he was, Axe wasn't immune to weapon fire.

"I haven't stolen Amun. He chose me."

"So you say. Too bad you're sleeping with the only person who could verify that. Dr. Rey has made one poor decision after another since arriving here. I'll be sure to convey my concerns to the oversight committee. Could you let her know that? It would set my mind at ease if you would."

She hissed and clenched her free hand into a fist. "Such an asshole."

Thanks to Hera, Rin saw Axe's jaw clench and his shoulders tighten. If Douglas didn't stop talking, this would blow up like a supernova.

"Of course. That way she'll have time to draft up a rebuttal to all your lies." Axe took another step. He was only a few meters away from Douglas, now. She'd seen Axe move and knew he was close enough he could cover the distance before the lieutenant could do anything.

"I said don't come any closer!" Douglas drew his blaster and aimed it at her lover.

After that, things happened too fast for her to track. One second Axe stood facing Douglas. The next, the lieutenant was on the ground with Axe's boot on his chest and his staff extended and pointed at Douglas's throat. The lieutenant's weapon lay a few meters away, too far for Douglas to reach.

"Do. Not. Move." Axe's commanding voice rumbled with the power of an avalanche. Without looking away from Douglas, Axe raised his voice and added, "And no one else do anything stupid. Your lieutenant is an idiot, but he was right about one thing. I *am* one of the most dangerous weapons in the galaxy."

Rin shivered, a response that had nothing to do with the tension of the moment and everything to do with the sudden spike of lust that slammed into her without warning. *Not now*, she told herself. *You can go gooey over the badass cyborg later.*

The others had a different reaction to Axe's warning. They lowered their weapons.

"Take him down!" Douglas yelled. "Why are you just standing there?"

"Because they're smarter than you," Axe snarled. "And none of them want to die today."

Douglas kept blustering. "He's alone! You *fraxxing* cowards are a disgrace to the uniform."

Rin decided to join the conversation. She rose into view, making sure everyone could see the plasma pistol she held. "Actually, he's not alone. And for the record, Lieutenant, I think you are a bigger disgrace to that uniform."

"How the hell are you here?" Douglas lifted his head to stare at her, which earned him a poke with Axe's staff.

"Don't move," Axe reminded him.

"I'm a fast healer," she replied. "Now, where are Subjects Four and Six?"

"They never made it back to camp. Your bad decisions cost the program both—hnggh." His sentence ended with a wheeze as Axe pressed down on his chest.

"We know that's not true. They made it back here

safely, which means they were in your care when they vanished. You either lost them or did something to them. Either way, I want to know." Rin channeled all her anger into her words, which helped keep her voice steady and strong despite how worried she was.

"How could you possibly know they made it back?" Douglas's voice was a raspy wheeze, but she heard him well enough.

"The subjects are psychically linked. Testing the extent of that link was one of the reasons for this mission. It turns out they can stay connected for more than the kilometer we confirmed previously."

"That's not in your reports," Douglas whined.

Rin saw an opportunity and took it. "You mean it wasn't in the daily summaries I submitted to you. You only saw what I wanted you to see."

"That's what you think. I saw the drone footage. They used coordinated, strategic attacks against the drones. Those creatures are weapons of war, and you want to treat them like *pets*!"

"No, Lieutenant. I want to treat them like intelligent, sentient beings."

"Then you're a fool. Do you know what even a sample of their DNA is worth?"

Axe growled. "You want to enslave them the same way the corporations tried to enslave cyborgs like me. They're not property to be used or sold. Now for the last time, Lieutenant. Where are the missing psy-hawks?"

Sutherland spoke up. "They're in the shuttle already. We slipped them some knock-out gas while they were asleep and removed two from their cages before the others woke up. They're in cryo-pods. I saw two more pods in the same section. Could be more of them."

"You backstabbing bastard," Douglas said, glaring.

"This was your idea from the beginning. We signed on because you promised us an easy assignment with a big payday for almost no risk." Sutherland gestured around them. "Then we get sent to the ass-end of nowhere and aren't even allowed to set foot in the one and only town on the whole planet."

"Shut up. You're ruining everything." Douglas sounded more like a toddler having a tantrum than a grown man.

"I figure this is my chance to get out of the shit you got us into." He looked over to Rin and shrugged. "I'll cooperate. You want to know the details? I'll give them to you. Someone out there wanted those birds of yours and they were going to pay us a fortune to get them. It was all planned, but then we got sent here and the lieutenant had to figure out a way to make it right with the client or we were all going to get the blame." Sutherland shrugged. "I don't know who they are, but they're dangerous. Some of the things they threatened to do if we didn't come through..." The soldier shuddered.

"Shut up. Shut up! Shut up! They'll kill us all if you keep talking, you idiot!"

"Who will?" Axe demanded.

"*Fraxx* you, machine."

Axe removed his boot from Douglas's chest, bent down, and grabbed him by the front of his uniform. Then Axe hauled him into the air so Douglas's feet hung in the air. "Want to try that again?"

"*Fraxx* off."

Rin didn't see Douglas pull the second blaster. It seemed to materialize in his hand between one heartbeat and the next. Axe didn't seem to notice it either.

At the same time, Amun dropped out of the sky and streaked like a meteor straight at Douglas's head. The collision stunned everyone—the hawk, the human, and the cyborg.

Amun crashed to the ground, too dazed to pull himself out of the dive while Douglas tried to wipe the blood flowing into his eyes from his newly lacerated scalp.

Axe looked away from his prisoner to check on Amun, and in that moment Douglas raised his weapon... and Rin fired.

The man's head vanished in a pinkish cloud of vaporized tissue. Rin trained her weapon on the nearest soldier, but all he did was raise his hands and take a step back. The others did the same thing. No one seemed overly upset that she'd just killed their commanding officer. Maybe they didn't like him that much after all.

Axe snapped his head around to stare at the dead body dangling from his hand.

"Nice shot, sunshine!" he called over. Then he dropped the corpse onto the ground and hurried over to Amun.

"Is he okay?" she asked.

Hera sent her a pulse of affirmation at the same moment Axe held up a fist, thumb up. "He'll be fine."

Rin exhaled and suddenly had to plant a hand on the side of the sled to stop her knees from giving out. They'd done it. She had no idea how to make sure that the hawks would never be exploited or abused again, but she knew they'd find a way to make that happen, too.

She and Axe were a team, and so much more. She was his sunshine... and he was her everything.

EPILOGUE

Axe sat in a beam of autumn sunshine, watching the psy-hawks as they soared in lazy circles overhead. Rin lay beside him, her head and neck resting on his thigh.

"Do you think they're as happy as we are?" she asked, pointing a finger at the sky.

He chuckled. "I know they are. Amun keeps sending me the psychic version of smiling emojis. It's annoying as hell, and he knows it. Damned bird."

These days what little grumbling he did was all for show. Over the last few months he'd come to realize that he'd grumbled mostly to have a reason to speak aloud, even if no one else was around to hear him. It was one of the ways he'd tried to stave off feelings of loneliness, but that wasn't necessary anymore. He had Rin and the hawks to talk to, and Amun was always just a thought away.

They even had visitors from time to time. He'd discovered that cooking for other people was gratifying in ways he couldn't articulate, and he'd come to enjoy their dinner parties. But only once a month.

Despite that rule, Rin had somehow talked him into hosting an open house of sorts. The entire colony was invited to drop by for a weekend-long social to learn more about the psy-hawks. She'd even convinced him to put some of his work on display. He'd only agreed when she promised that Anya and the staff at the Bar None tavern had offered to cater the event.

Mostly, he'd agreed because it would give the hawks a chance to meet more of the colonists. So far, only Amun and Hera had bonded with anyone. Rin hoped to change that.

For now, all eight of the birds stayed with them. Amun and Hera shared the workshop while he'd built the others an open-style mews with multiple roosts and access points. They were free to come and go as they pleased, which was a far cry from their previous existence.

It took some time for them to adjust to their new reality. Axe understood all too well what it was like to transition from captivity and slavery to a life of freedom. It took even longer for the four hawks Douglas had put into cryo-pods. When they'd boarded the shuttle to track down the missing subjects, they'd found the two that had been taken that morning and the two the lieutenant claimed had been left behind. Rin had been both heartbroken and furious at the discovery.

All four had short-term health issues from being placed in cryo without any of the standard preparations and procedures, but Rin had diligently nursed them back to full health. Now they were recovered, it was time for the birds to meet the rest of the colony's citizens.

After what Douglas had done, the IAF had no choice but to give in to Rin's demands that the hawks be allowed to stay on Haven. It helped that the local council backed Rin, and they even called in a few favors with other agencies to ensure the hawks would have permanent protection and recognition as a sentient species. Nova Force even got involved at one point. They ensured that every scrap of information was scrubbed from the record except for a single copy that was handed over to Haven's council. It meant no one would be able to create more psy-hawks or use the data for anything else.

"Did I tell you I heard from Jade this morning?" Rin asked.

"You didn't, but as I recall, you didn't say much of anything when I came in for lunch." He laughed as he remembered seeing her walk into the kitchen gloriously naked and offering herself up as the main course.

Rin reached up to pat his leg. "Is that a complaint?"

"*Fraxx* no. No complaints at all, sunshine." He caught her hand in his and held on to it.

"So, what did our non-royal cyber-jockey have to say?"

Rin snickered. "She hates it when you call her that, and so does the princess."

"Not my fault we have two people with the same skill set. How else am I supposed to differential between them?"

"You could use their names, you difficult man."

"Difficult *cyborg*. No need to get insulting."

"Very difficult cyborg. And Jade said the encryption on the project's files was the best she's ever seen, but she's making progress. She's got the name of the scientist who started the psy-hawk project."

That got his attention. "Who was it?"

"I've never heard of him before, but Jade said the council was alarmed when they heard the name."

"What name?" he asked, hoping she said any name but one.

"Dr. Jules Absalom. Do you know who that is?"

Fraxx. Of course it would be him. "I know the name, and what he's done. Jules Absalom was an evil, soulless bastard. He's the one who created the cyborg program and was involved with the original theft of the DNA from the Vault of the Fallen. He also unleashed a fully sentient AI into the galaxy, experimented on cyborgs after the wars ended, and was wanted for an entire laundry list of illegal acts until his death last year."

Rin sat up. "Holy hell. So there's no doubt that he intended to use the hawks the same way he ended up using the cyborgs?"

"None at all. And now we know that, we can make a solid guess as to who was trying to buy the hawks from Douglas."

Rin nodded. "I've heard the rumors. It could have been one of the corporations, but you think it's the group calling themselves the Shadows. Don't you?"

"I do."

Worry creased Rin's face, and he knew he needed to do something to reassure her. He tugged at her hand until she moved close enough he could draw her into his lap and then kissed her several times.

"What do we do now? How do we protect the hawks?" she asked.

"They are under the same protections as the rest of the colony," he reminded her. "They're even recognized as citizens. If trouble comes, we'll fight to defend our home and *everyone* living here."

She blew out a breath and nodded slowly. "You make it sound so simple."

He caught her face in his hands and smiled down at her, still amazed that this woman had chosen him. "It is simple, sunshine. Love is always worth fighting for. I love you and the life we're building here, and I will fight to my last breath to keep it."

She leaned into his arms with a sigh that morphed into a burble of laughter. "I love you, too. I just hope we don't have to fight anyone to prove it."

"Me too, sunshine. Me too." Even as he said it, Axe knew it wouldn't be that easy. Trouble would come to Haven eventually. When it did, they'd have to be ready... and enjoy every minute together until that day came.

***

Thank you for reading Her Cyborg Lumberjack.

I hope you enjoyed Axe and Rin's story.
Would you like to read a special bonus epilogue to this story? Sign up for my newsletter here:

<u>subscribepage.io/Bonuscontent</u>

If you're looking for more stories like this one, I invite you to explore the other books in the <u>Drift</u> universe, which now Include Haven Colony, <u>Nova Force</u> and the original <u>Drift</u> series.

ABOUT THE AUTHOR

Susan lives out on the Canadian west coast surrounded by open water, dear family, and good friends. She's jumped out of perfectly good airplanes on purpose and accidentally swum with sharks on the Great Barrier Reef.

If the world ends, she plans to survive as the spunky, comedic sidekick to the heroes of the new world, because she's too damned short and out of shape to make it on her own for long.

You can find out more about Susan and her books at:
www.susanhayes.ca